Words of Assurance
to the Wise

Words of Assurance to the Wise

Volume I

Irvin J. Rickey, Sr.

VANTAGE PRESS
New York

Published by Vantage Press, Inc.
516 West 34th Street, New York, New York 10001

Manufactured in the United States of America
ISBN: 0-533-14078-1

Library of Congress Catalog Card No.: 01-126947

0 9 8 7 6 5 4 3 2 1

Contents

Words of Assurance
to the Wise

The Right Choice

In this life could I choose
One talent above the rest,
One to keep and not to lose,
Would I choose the best?

Were a vocal talent given me
So I could express my feelings in song,
Would my voice in faultless harmony
Sing the Saviour's praises loud and long?

Were a musical talent by Jesus sent
So beautiful music I could make,
Would my talent to God be lent
Or would His cause I forsake?

With great wisdom were I endowed,
Would I make the right choice?
If my complete freedom were allowed,
Would I heed Christ's or Satan's voice?

Were unlimited power my possession,
With wisdom would I rule?
Or would it become a vain obsession
And my reign that of a fool?

Were an artistic talent a celestial gift
And my paintings superb and fine,
From Christ's service would I drift,
Would worldly selfishness be mine?

Although there swells within me
The wish for a talent supreme,
For this desire I make no plea
To Christ Jesus, Lord and King.

In the years God has graciously lent,
I have confessed my weakness and sin,
Placing my faith in the Christ God sent,
Trusting Him that Salvation I'll win.

So you see my choice has been made,
In Christ Jesus I have peace of mind;
I face the future and Eternity unafraid,
Certain superior talents in Heaven I'll find.

Christ Jesus, Creator of Beauty

Sunrise, with brilliant rays of light
Sunset, with clouds of burnished gold,
The full moon rising on a cloudless night
Whose golden glow is beautiful to behold.

An ocean tide with white and foaming spray,
A redwood forest with trees straight and tall,
A mountain trail with flowers along the way,
Which leads to a mighty waterfall.

A secluded hidden lake, deep and still
Whose waters mirror adjacent mountains high,
A trickling spring which vainly tries to fill
The silent, wandering stream flowing by.

Spring, with its myriad moving flowers,
Summer, with its fields of grain bent low,
Autumn, with its chilling rain showers,
Winter, with earth covered by falling snow.

These creations of beauty Christ Jesus made
Each shows forth His mighty power,
Yet, the beauty of each will some day fade
Like that of a fragile flower.

Christ Jesus has a gift to give,
A gift that will not age or fade,
Those trusting Him forever will live
In Heaven's mansions that He has made.

Jesus Was There

Pursuing life's temporal fame,
I lived a life of sin and shame
Yet, Christ at Calvary took my blame;
Jesus was there.

Things of the world I eagerly sought;
In Satan's web I was securely caught
And though my life seemed for naught,
Jesus was there.

Into my life the "Spirit" came,
Convicting me of my sin's shame
And when in faith I called His Name,
Jesus was there.

From the Devil's grasp I was torn:
As God's child I was miraculously won
And with help Satan's ways to scorn,
Jesus was there.

Since that happy eventful day
When God His grace did display
With help to guide me on my way,
Jesus was there.

In my life's ensuing years
Thru its bitter flowing tears
With help to calm my fears,
Jesus was there.

When danger met me in life's race
And I desired a saner safer place,
With a fresh supply of His grace,
Jesus was there.

If you desire Salvation and peace of mind
And would that God to your sins were blind,
Trust Christ as Saviour and you will find
Jesus is there.

No Greater Love

No greater love can we recall
As we search our history
Than that of Christ who gave His all
On the cross of Calvary.

No greater love was ever shown
Than Christ has shown so free
As He suffered, bled and died alone
Upon that rugged tree.

No greater love than Christ's we know
Will ever be known to man
And by that love His blood did flow
For God's Redemption Plan.

No greater love can stir a heart
And may our love for Him
Be shown as we do our part
By trying the "lost" to win.

No greater love, Christ is the Way,
We hear this heavenly call;
Believe on Him, confess today;
Give Him your life, your all.

God's Great Love

As a firefly's light in Carlsbad Cave,
As a drop of water in a tidal wave,
As a single hill in this world He gave
I'm surrounded by God's Great Love.

From the drop of a pin to a tornado's roar,
From the height of an ant to an eagle's soar,
From the depth of a pond to the ocean's floor
I'm amazed by the power of God's Great Love.

As a single flake in a winter's snow,
As a gentle breeze in a hurricane's blow,
As a trickling spring in Niagara's flow
I'm surrounded by God's Great Love.

From a minnow's flight to a salmon run,
From a firecracker's noise to an atomic gun,
From a lantern's light to the mighty sun
I'm amazed by the power of God's Great Love.

As a grain of sand in the desert wide,
As a broken pebble on the Great Divide,
As a drop of foam on the ocean tide
I'm surrounded by God's Great Love.

From a mesquite bush to a forest tall,
From a rippling creek to a waterfall,
From a furrow in the earth to Grand Canyon's wall
I'm amazed by the power of God's Great Love.

Above all the wonders of our world so wide
God's boundless Love flows like a tide;
To those who willingly come to His Side
Through Jesus, the Son of our God.

Our Saviour's Love

Love o'erwhelming, love divine,
Love unequaled or surpassed,
Love unchanging, pure and fine,
Love unceasing, first and last.

Love of mercy, grace revealing,
Love unbounded, fair and just,
Love amazing, for faith appealing,
Love so constant, worthy of trust.

Love so precious, love of power,
Love so spotless, sincere and kind,
Love sufficient, a sheltering tower,
Love that gives one peace of mind.

Love so rapturous, brave yet meek,
Love so righteous, faithful and true,
Love of compassion led Christ to seek
God's Holy Will in His life to do.

Our perfect Saviour atonement has made
By His willing death on Calvary's tree;
His flawless life sin's ransom has paid
That each Believer on Earth might be free.

Christ Jesus our Saviour is God's Holy Son,
His love led Him to die in man's place;
The Bible reveals that Salvation is won
By faith in Christ, a gift of God's Grace.

Christ's Love

Love supreme and time defying
Is available to the "lost,"
Love divine and never dying
Still is offered without cost.

Love to conquer every care,
Free to those who need it most,
Love that promises heavenly fare,
The love of which Angels boast.

Love, life's trying years to span
Is offered mortals one and all,
Love to save each needy man
To prevent his fatal fall.

Love, God's true expression of grace
Is extended to sinful man;
Love, doubts and fears will replace
For all who accept God's Plan.

Love for Time and Eternity too,
Love that cannot be bound,
Love unfailing, unmeasurable and true,
This love in Christ is found.

Love to strengthen a faltering heart,
Love to soothe a troubled mind,
Love that only God can impart,
Love that all in Christ may find.

Love that will survive the test of time,
Love that only God could conceive,
Love that brings rewards sublime
To those by faith whom Christ receive.

By the Touch of the Master's Hand

From the abyss of endless space,
From a heavenly home of grace
Came One to bless the human race
By the touch of the Master's Hand.

From Heaven's realm Christ Jesus came,
Renouncing throne and celestial fame
To bring Salvation from sin and shame
By the touch of the Master's Hand.

Christ Jesus came in time of need;
He came man's hungry soul to feed,
Showing God's love by word and deed
By the touch of the Master's Hand.

The sick of soul in Him could find
Release from the sins that bind
And light was given to the blind
By the touch of the Master's Hand.

To a withered hand new strength came
As to the legs of the halt and lame
And the "lost" was absolved from blame
By the touch of the Master's Hand.

The leper's skin became fresh and new;
Control was placed on winds that blew
And on the sea that the disciples knew
By the touch of the Master's Hand.

These miracles men were allowed to see
From Satan they were admonished to flee
And from life's burdens they were made free
By the touch of the Master's Hand.

Each soul must choose an abiding place;
The "lost" thru eternity his sin must face,
Knowing God offered him Redeeming Grace
By the touch of the Master's Hand.

Christmas, God's Gift to Man

The golden bells of Heaven chime
Every year at Christmastime,
Recalling the joyous news sublime
The Angel gave to mortals.

Shepherds watching flocks at night
Were startled by a wondrous sight,
Transfixed and trembling in fright
At the visitor from heaven's portals.

"Fear not," came the reassuring sound,
"God has planned that joy shall abound,
For tonight in Bethlehem may be found
The Messiah of God's Plan."

The shepherds the angelic voice obeyed
Grateful that God's message conveyed;
News of Him for whom they had prayed
Christ Jesus, the Saviour of man.

Hurrying to Bethlehem that very night,
The shepherds shared a marvelous sight
That filled each viewer with delight
Christ Jesus, God's Gift from above.

They worshiped Christ and praises gave
To God for Him who came to save
Man from sin and the eternal grave,
God's revelation of redemptive love.

These signs a merciful God has shown,
Desiring that Christ His Son be known
Ere time for repentance has flown,
Bringing Judgment Day to all.

The blessed Saviour came that night;
He came to conquer wrong with right;
Are you with Him in His fight?
Have you heard and accepted His call?

God's Many Attributes

If in my mind I could conceive
God's wondrous mercy and grace,
Man's highest medal I should receive
If I revealed it to the human race.

If my eyes were allowed to behold
God's supreme purity and light,
Then perchance more could be told
Of a Believer's future home of delight.

If my ears were attuned to hear
The joyous sounds in heaven's halls,
Those sounds would allay my fear
And alert my senses to the Spirit's calls.

If with an artist's brush could be revealed
The true beauty of earth and sky,
God's great love would remain concealed
For human expression it does defy.

If one were to live a thousand years
Encouraging the "lost" their sin to repent,
This would surely diminish future tears
For some would trust the Saviour God sent.

If one could speak with an orator's tongue
And God's many attributes reveal,
These qualities by heaven's saints are sung;
Such traits are impossible to conceal.

These words now come to their inevitable end
As come to an end they must;
Their truth points to Christ, man's dearest Friend
Whom for Salvation mortals must trust.

The Fool

The fool in his ignorance has said
That God did not create mortal man;
Blindly by Satan fools are led
To disavow God's Creation Plan.

The fool does not know what Eternity holds
For those who do not trust in God's Son;
To his eternal horror as the future unfolds,
He will experience what his unbelief has won.

God does not condone the acts of a fool,
For man is the highest creation He made
Yet, many men serve Satan as a willing tool,
Their certain doom they shall not evade.

God sent His Holy Son to die for man,
Knowing man needed redemption from sin;
Showing faith in Christ Jesus is God's Plan
For mankind the gift of Salvation to win.

The fool in his ignorance lives day by day
Never pondering what the future holds;
His atheism and bravado are always on display
While his destined time on Earth unfolds.

What fools do not know will not prevent
The fate that is reserved for their kind;
After Judgment Day they will desire to repent,
Confessing to God's purposes they were blind.

Yet, their pleading voices will not deter
God's judgment and punishment of sin,
For each fool was given what he did prefer
And none chose the gift of Salvation to win.

Suppose

Suppose you knew what the future holds
As well as the past is known,
Where would you be as Time unfolds
And the age for Redemption has flown?

Suppose you knew what tomorrow would bring,
Would you turn it to profit or gain?
Or would you in loving service cling
To our Saviour Who was willingly slain?

Suppose you knew that friends would fail,
Would you have an understanding heart?
Or would you their failures assail
And in scathing criticism take part?

Suppose you knew the day you would die,
Would your witness terminate at the grave?
Is Jesus your Saviour or do you deny
That He is the only One who can save?

Suppose you knew the hours as well as the day
That Christ Jesus our Saviour will return,
Would your life be full of joy or dismay?
Would His return you welcome or spurn?

Suppose you could see our Saviour on high
Surrounded by an adoring host,
Will you be one who joins the in the sky
Claiming life's prize valued the most?

The Wise Men

Across the barren wastes they came
Following the shining star;
Some wise men we cannot name
Came to worship Christ from afar.

To biblical prophecies they were not blind
And when the Star appeared in the sky,
They were eager and determined to find
The promised revelation from on high.

To Jerusalem this group went
The newborn King of the Jews to find;
To Bethlehem they were sent
By King Herod who was spiritually blind.

They found the Lord Jesus there in a humble abode
And presented Him gifts that day;
They returned to their land by a different road
To Herod's bitter and angry dismay.

God warned Joseph that Herod was intent
On killing Christ Jesus the Saviour of man;
To Egypt Joseph, Mary and Jesus went
To prevent Herod from completing his plan.

Now our Lord and Saviour the wise men sought
Is available to mortals today;
He is ready to give the Salvation He bought
To all who accept Him as The Way.

Will you be as wise as those men of old
Who sought the Saviour the guiding star revealed?
Will the fact of your acceptance be told
When mortal life records are no longer concealed?

I See

I see the beauty of each day
That our God is pleased to give;
I see the Bible that reveals The Way
God wants Earth's mortals to live.

I see the temporal things of Earth
By the light of our shining Sun;
I see in the Bible a soul's worth
And Christ's victory over sin was won.

I see Earth's teeming mortals
Engrossed in seeking worldly gain;
I see them entering sinful portals
In whose power many choose to remain.

I see the "lost" who refuse to believe
That Eternal Salvation may be won;
I see in the Bible there is no reprieve
For those failing to accept God's Son.

I see a gracious God extending man's time
In weeks and months and years;
I see in the Bible Heaven's rewards sublime
In the absence of troubles and tears.

I see a future day facing mortal man
When each shall reap what was sown;
I see some reflecting the Salvation Plan,
Which God in mercy has made known.

I see in the Bible our Saviour and Friend
With rewards which only He could make;
I see the fate of Earth's mortals depend
Upon which of life's two paths they take.

Heaven's Door

As water fills each restless sea
Until they lash at each restraining shore,
God offered grace man could see
By sending His Son to be Heaven's Door.

Our eternal God knew the plight of man,
He was aware of man's greatest need;
God sent His Son to complete His Plan
And Christ Jesus completed the deed.

Now, our Saviour is in Heaven above
Interceding for weak mortal man;
The Holy Spirit reveals God's love,
Convincing men to accept God's Plan.

Many Believers have reached Heaven's shore
By accepting God's Redemption Plan,
Placing their trust in Christ as Heaven's Door
Since He is the only Saviour for man.

For those who have yet to believe
That God expects mortals to repent,
They must know there is no reprieve
For those rejecting the Saviour God sent.

Our perfect Saviour has provided the way
To Heaven's promised treasures above;
Those who desire with Him there to stay
Must accept God's offer of love.

God is merciful and extends His grace
By providing sinful mortals more time;
Time their doubts and fears to replace
With faith in Christ for rewards sublime.

I Believe

I believe long ago our Saviour came
To reveal God's concern and care;
I believe Jesus and trust in His Name
And hope His eternal abode to share.

I believe our God is Great and Just,
His mercy is without known bounds;
I believe God sent Jesus for us to trust
While His grace toward mankind abounds.

I believe that Christ Jesus is The Way
To Heaven's eternal realms above;
I believe our Saviour will return one day
To receive those who return His love.

I believe that God has extended His grace
So Earth's mortals will have time to choose;
The Bible reveals hell as the abiding place
Of those whom their eternal souls do lose.

I believe that mortals should not waste time
Nor trust their future to Fate;
Only the Trinity offers rewards sublime
In a blissful eternal state.

I believe that God will send His Son
To receive those who have made Him their choice;
Heaven's eternal blessings may be won
By those persons who heed God's warning voice.

I believe that our Saviour we shall soon see
With His accompanying host in the sky;
Together with Him Earth's saved shall flee
To an abode all description does defy.

Mine

God's greatest gift is mine,
Which was purchased by His Son;
Eternal life, this gift sublime
By faith in Christ Jesus is won.

God's gift of Time is mine;
It alone is God's to give;
Christ Jesus, God's Son Divine,
Has shown us how to live.

God's gift of health is mine,
Which mortals do not deserve
And He reserves mansions fine
For those in His Will who serve.

God's gift of grace also is mine,
Which He freely bestows on man
And God desires as Time's years decline
That Earth's mortals will accept His Plan.

God's mercy assuredly is mine
And by His goodness I have been blessed;
God's mercy does not decline
To those whom His Son have confessed.

God's provisions surely are mine,
Which He delights to bestow;
His ear to my prayers does incline
While blessings from Him daily flow.

God's love also is mine,
Which He with all Believers does share;
A Christian's attributes He does refine
To prepare them for eternal heavenly fare.

Christ the Saviour Came to Earth

Christ the Saviour came to earth
One cold and wintry night;
The angels announcing His royal birth
Were bathed in a heavenly light.

Their songs of gladness filled the air
Of good will to men and peace on earth;
They sang of Bethlehem; the Holy Child there
And of His truly miraculous birth.

The shepherds who saw this wondrous sight
Felt an inner spiritual lift
And hurried to Bethlehem that very night
To see this Greatest Gift.

There in a manger the Saviour lay,
Under watchful eyes He peacefully slept;
The joyous shepherds knelt to pray,
Thanking God for His promise kept.

We were not there nor did we see
The blessed Saviour's birth
But we know He lives to keep us free
From Satan's power on earth.

May we, like the angelic hosts above,
Praise God for His Holy Son
By telling others of Christ's love
And the victory over sin He won.

Christ the Saviour and You

Do you work for Christ Jesus
Or do you work for self?
Do you read the Bible daily
Or leave it on the shelf?

Are you active in His service
On Sunday and weekdays too?
Or do you find a greater pleasure
In the worldly things you do?

Have you trusted Christ as Saviour?
Are you a witness to the "lost"?
Do you consistently try to serve Him
No matter what the cost?

Are you waiting for His kingdom?
Are you eager for the rest
That you'll take in Heaven with Jesus
And with others who pass God's test?

Do you faithfully look for His coming
Carried triumphantly by clouds on high?
Coming to call His Saints to rest
In their new home beyond the sky?

If your heart beats faster
At the thought of His return,
Then acknowledge Him as Master
And help others His love to learn.

Christ's Mission and Fulfillment

The epoch day Christ Jesus died
On Calvary's desolate hill,
His blood flowed a crimson tide
Till Death His lips did still.

The painful wounds, the open shame
Christ Jesus willingly bore;
Hence God chose His wondrous Name
As the Key to Heaven's door.

While Christ suffered on the tree,
Few friends were standing near,
For abject fear had caused to flee
Many friends whom He held dear.

Among the faithful waiting few
Were the ones who loved Him best;
These true friends the Saviour knew
Would pass this loyalty test.

The unbelieving scoffers came
Hurling taunts in the Saviour's face,
Reviling Him who took the blame
Of the sinful human race.

One dying thief was heard to rail
"Save us all if you're God's Son,"
But Christ knew that He would fail
If this miracle were done.

The other thief was heard to say,
"In your kingdom, Lord, remember me."
Christ honored his prayer that day
And took him to Paradise from Calvary.

As Christ for man willingly died,
The veil in the Temple was rent;
And the Sun in grief its face did hide
As Christ's ebbing blood was spent.

Loving hands laid Christ's body to rest
In Joseph's tomb, a compassionate man
As broken hearts forgot the final test
Christ must pass in the Salvation Plan.

By order of law the grave was sealed,
A stone placed at the door to remain;
His enemies remembered that Christ revealed
On the third day He would rise again.

Early Easter morn Disciples came to the tomb
And found the stone rolled away;
Christ's grave clothes were left in the room
On this glorious Resurrection Day.

The Saviour had risen true to His word,
Winning victory over Death and Sin;
He charged His disciples and all who heard
The "lost" of the world to win.

Lord Jesus, Our Sustainer

Lord Jesus, in Nature we see Thy hand
And in each creation Thy power;
By your will the mountains stand
As does each tree and flower.

By your grace the Sun does shine
To warm this temporal earth,
Conceived and created by Thy power divine,
Who can determine its worth?

The stars and planets readily show
The genius of Thy mind,
For by their presence man may know
Thou art not hard to find.

Lord Jesus, the provision Thou hast wrought
Surround us on every hand,
Inconceivable in value, in bounty brought
To the mortals of every land.

The food, the shelter Thou dost provide
For the unworthy human race,
Reveals to man Thy love does abide
Exceeded only by Thy grace.

Lord Jesus, much we need Thy tender care,
For Satan rules earth with his host,
Yet, with Thy aid and Thy generous fare,
We have what is needed most.

Lord, for Thy immeasurable love and grace,
We give our heartfelt thanks to Thee;
We pray that soon we shall see Thy face
And to Thy eternal abode we shall flee.

Jesus

Jesus, the Name of the Saviour God sent,
Jesus, the creator in His own right,
Jesus, who urges lost sinners to repent
Who can redeem them from their plight.

Jesus, who laid aside His celestial fame
To reveal God's love and grace to man,
Jesus, the Name of the blessed One who came
To complete God's only Salvation Plan.

Jesus, the lamb of God who was slain,
Jesus, who tasted death for Earth's mortals,
Jesus, whose sacrifice was not in vain
Is now preparing mansions in heaven's portals.

Jesus, the One whom Death could not hold,
Jesus, who made a mockery of the grave,
Jesus, who has power and wealth untold,
Jesus, ever willing Earth's sinners to save.

Jesus, God's Son who lived on this planet Earth
A dedicated life, sinless and pure,
Jesus, who made possible man's Second Birth
And by whose power it will forever endure.

Jesus, who now in heaven does abide,
Is preparing to return to this earth;
He will come in power to claim His Bride,
Those who have experienced their Second Birth.

Jesus, this warning to mortals would make,
Be ready although the date of His coming is concealed,
Only those who are prepared will He take;
Daily let your loving service for Him be revealed.

Lord Jesus

Although I cannot see Your face
Nor Your voice can I hear,
You shower me with love and grace
And I feel that You are near.

Many times my mind does dwell
On Your handiwork here on Earth,
The beauty of each creation seems to tell
Of its special primordial birth.

The exquisite beauty of a secluded lake
Cradled in luxury by countless trees
Is there for Earth's mortals to take,
Yet, time for enjoyment quickly flees.

The grandeur of snow-capped mountains tall
Causes the weak mortal mind to wonder
Why such a creator willingly gave His all
To redeem mortals ere Time is cut asunder.

Lord Jesus, mankind has yet to conceive
The magnitude of Your grace;
You purchased Salvation mortals can receive
Since You freely died in their place.

Lord Jesus, accept my humble thanks today
For life's blessings You enable me to share;
May the Holy Spirit through my life display
My gratitude for Your protective care.

Lord Jesus, we on Earth long to see
You and Your countless host in space;
With You to heaven we will gladly flee
As we're anxious to see that glorious place.

Faith in the Saviour

Today I dream of that tomorrow
When the joys of Heaven I'll know
And from this vision I can borrow
Strength to live on this Earth below.

Again I dream of future days
When Time from Earth has fled
And the reward that Faith pays
To each Christian, Spirit-led.

In life Christians must fight
And each victory that is won
Against the prince of eternal night
Is championed by God's Son.

Against the flailing fists of Time
Against Eternity's surging tide,
I put a Saviour's love divine;
Safe in His love I shall abide.

Against Satan and his callous band,
Against days with perils fraught,
With faith in Christ I stand
Firm against their fierce onslaught.

If your life too is under stress,
If you wish for the Saviour's aid,
Have faith in Christ when troubles press
And you can face the future unafraid.

Faith

Foremost among the traits of man
Faith stands above all the rest,
For through faith God has a Plan
By which mortals pass life's test.

Faith makes it possible for man to receive
All the worthwhile blessings of life;
Faith is a quality difficult to deceive,
It never wavers in times of strife.

Faith is a gift from our Creator above
And through it rewards may be won,
Faith makes available God's Gift of Love,
Which is the Salvation found in His Son.

Faith causes the spiritual blind to see,
Faith makes the doubters believe,
Faith exercised from sin sets free
Mortals whom God will now receive.

Faith guides man to become true and just;
It keeps God's way his way;
For those seeking Salvation faith is a must;
It should be on continual display.

Faith is a quality that begets love;
It's never content to sleep,
It points the lost to Christ above
And God's laws it endeavors to keep.

Faith is available to the mortals of Earth,
It should be used to accept God's Son;
In Christ Jesus alone is the Second Birth;
There's no other way eternal life may be won.

God's Grace

God's grace permeates this world,
It confronts us on every hand;
It's as visible as a flag unfurled
To the Christians of Christ's band.

God's supreme gift of grace
Was the sacrifice of His Son
Whose death in mortal man's place
Made Salvation available to be won.

The air we breathe, the food we eat
And the precious rain God causes to fall
Are gifts of grace we savor sweet
And we praise God for them one and all.

We thank God for the life-preserving rays of the Sun,
Which brings warmth causing plants to grow;
We thank God for the soul-preserving gift of His Son
Whom, with the Holy Spirit's help we can know.

We thank God for our Church and Christian friends
And for the family God graciously gave;
We thank God that His grace with mercy blends
And that mankind He continues to save.

We thank God because of His abundant grace
That our home with Him is assured;
Even now Christ Jesus is preparing the place
For those who a saving faith has secured.

We thank God for His mercy, grace and love
Manifested in His Salvation Plan;
We thank Him for prepared mansions above
Which He will share with redeemed man.

His Love Is Enough for Me

His love is like the eternal spring
His love for all rich blessings bring
His love is the anchor to which I cling
His love is enough for me.

His love is true as love should be
His love led Him to Calvary
His love made Him endure the tree
His love is enough for me.

His love for all the world was shown
His love is the greatest ever known
His love will justify His own
His love is enough for me.

His love made Him our sin debt pay
His love has shown us the Christian Way
His love is still alive today
His love is enough for me.

His love conceived the Salvation Plan
His love brought it down to man
His love a mighty gulf did span
His love is enough for me.

His love is shown by His pleading call
His love demands our life, our all
His love will hold us so we cannot fall
His love is enough for me.

A Prayer for Power

Lord Jesus, when I Thy glory see
With others whom Thou didst free
There, engulfed by Thy Eternity
Our tongues Thy praise shall sing.

Within Heaven there is no night;
Thy radiant glory provides the light,
Revealing scenes of utter delight
Which You created, our King.

Yet Lord, here on this Earth
We who received the Second Birth
Will not comprehend its true worth
Until we see Thy Face.

Now Lord, we are in a plight,
Engaged in a desperate fight
With the ruler of Eternal Night;
We need Thy power and grace.

Grant Lord, that we may
Live for You day by day,
Help us witness, work and pray
Until You call us home.

Then Lord, until that hour
Fill us with Thy love and power
And may Thy mercy like a shower
On weak mortal man be shown.

My Prayer

Gracious Saviour, attend this plea
Extend Thy blessings now to me;
Help me bear my service cross;
Purify my heart and purge its dross.

Gracious Saviour, to me draw near
Dispel my doubts and calm my fear;
Fill me with a deeper love,
Fit me for Thy home above.

Gracious Saviour, extend Thy hand
To protect me from Satan's band,
For evil rears its ugly head
To thwart Christians, Spirit-led.

Gracious Saviour, fill my heart
With a love that I may impart
To the lost, the spiritually blind
That they Thy will might find.

Gracious Saviour, lead my feet
In paths of victory, not defeat
And may I by Thy strength impart
Hope to some faltering heart.

Gracious Saviour, hear my call;
Grant that I shall never fall
To Satan's wiles nor his will seek
Nor in his favor my lips speak.

Gracious Saviour, ere this prayer end
Grant Thy Spirit shall further lend,
Grace to live and boldness to speak
Of Thy Salvation men should seek.

A Prayer

Lord Jesus, omnipotent and divine,
May Thy celestial ways be mine;
Fill my heart with renewed love
For Thee and Thy kingdom above.

Lord Jesus, wilt Thou in mercy impart
Faith and strength to my faint heart;
Lord, I also ask Thee my life to lead
And for Thy continuing blessings I plead.

Lord Jesus, wilt Thou this prayer hear:
Grant salvation to those I hold dear,
Those whom Satan has securely caught
Lest their lives be lived for naught.

Lord Jesus, Satan has great power;
He is winning many battles this hour;
May Thy love and mercy hold sway
And may Thy will be done each day.

Lord Jesus, I pray that Your grace
My selfish acts and desires replace;
I pray for knowledge that I might win
Many lost souls who now delight in sin.

Lord Jesus, Thy divinity I again confess
And ask that Thou may witness bless;
Lord, those whom Satan causes to wait
Help me to them Your warning relate.

Lord Jesus, as surely as Satan's coming defeat,
Those trusting in You will savor sweet
The blessings given by the Father and Son
To those whose faith heaven's prize has won.

Another Prayer to God

O God, our Father, we adore Thee,
Thou art our Comfort and ready Aid;
In Thy continuing beneficence we see
Thy mercy and grace has not been stayed.

In self-denying love Thy precious Son came
So sinful mankind from sin could be saved;
Eternal Salvation is found in His Name
While the road to hell with others names is paved.

Lord God, we pray the Holy Spirit will guide
Our footsteps along the path of Right;
May we in Thy perfect will always abide
To repel attacks by the Prince of Night.

Lord God, we thank Thee for Thy continuing love
Manifested by Your gift of Time;
We look forward to a heavenly home above
Being created by our Saviour Divine.

Lord God, we praise Thee for each precious day
And the sustenance Thy Hand does provide;
May the mercy toward mortals You daily display,
Help the wayward on Christ to decide.

Lord God, we pray the Holy Spirit will strive
To help the "lost" trust in Christs Name
Ere the day of Judgment does suddenly arrive,
Bringing doom to those living in sin and shame.

Lord God, our minds cannot conceive the praise
Mankind owes to the Trinity above
But, to Thee our thankful voices we now raise
For Thy eternal and matchless love.

The Attributes of God

Love Divine and never waning
Love Supreme and always near
Love Complete and all sustaining
Love Omnipotent dispelling fear.

Love for mortals one and all
Love that begot Redeeming Grace
Love available to those who call
On Christ Jesus and seek His face.

Mercy that knows no end
Mercy available and sure
Mercy shown by man's Friend
Mercy unlimited and pure.

Mercy only God could create
Mercy needed by man's fall
Mercy that promises an estate
For saved mortals one and all.

Grace that cannot be earned
Grace that cannot be bought
Grace that the fool has spurned
Who in Satan's net is caught.

Grace that mortals yet may find
Grace for those who only hope
Grace the saved to Christ shall bind
Lest they in His service grope.

Unlimited love God conceived for man
With mercy and a time of reprieve;
Gracious Jesus, completing God's Plan
Offers salvation by faith man can receive.

Words of Praise

Lord God, Omnipotent and Divine
Through Christ Thy habitation is mine
Whose surroundings unbelievably sublime
Are abodes for Believers one and all.

Lord God, Sustainer of the human race
Author of Thy Salvation Plan of grace
In Thy mercy each Christian has a place
Behind Heaven's eternal jasper wall.

Lord God, thank Thee for Thy love
For the Saviour You sent from above,
Whom the Holy Spirit like a dove
Showed to man, Thy Perfect Son.

Lord God, may my life show thanks to Thee
For Christ our Lord Who came to free;
Repentant sinners bidding them to flee
To His arms where Salvation is won.

Lord God, upon this planet called Earth;
Satan fights against those of the Second Birth,
Denying to the lost the value and worth
Of trusting Christ Jesus as King.

Lord, God, help Earth's Christians in their fight
Against Satan, the Prince of Night;
Grant that Satan their witness does not blight
As they to Thy throne converts bring.

Lord God, eternal ruler of all creation
Accept this poor mortal's inadequate ovation;
Thou Who looketh not on rank or station
Accept these words of ardent praise.

Lord God, we Earth's mortals deeply desire
To keep Thy Word in our hearts afire;
May we willingly do the things You require
And in love serve You our remaining days.

Pride

Among the traits of mortal man
And one that is often denied,
One that hinders God's purpose and plan
Is that common trait called pride.

Pride has many facets and faces,
It causes much suffering and pain;
Often good traits it disgraces
And its negative results remain.

Pride is a virtue if in the right vein
As in service to God and man,
It can enhance man's spiritual gain
If used to promote God's Plan.

Pride that seeks only selfish gain
And denies God's claim on man's time;
It then becomes a sin stain
Which was paid for by God's Son divine.

Pride that causes man to deny his sin
To ignore God's warning to repent,
This type of pride hell's torments will win
By refusing the Saviour God sent.

Which path has pride caused you to take?
Are you under God or Satan's spell?
God in mercy gives you time to make
Your eternal choice of heaven or hell.

Falling Fire
(2 Kings 1:1–18)

Elijah, God's prophet, sat on a hill
Below a captain and his fifty came;
Elijah was busy doing God's will
When the captain called his name.

"Elijah, thou man of God, come down
For this is King Ahaziah's desire."
Elijah ignored the threat of the crown
And the fifty-one were destroyed by fire.

A second captain and his fifty came
And repeated the King's desire;
Elijah spoke and the results were the same,
For these also were destroyed by fire.

A third captain and his fifty came near,
A plea for mercy did he wisely bring;
God commanded Elijah to answer without fear
And to convey God's message to the King.

God's message was that the King would soon die,
For the King had chosen a false god to serve;
May this be a warning as from heaven on high
To those tempted from God's service to swerve.

When?

When, Lord God, omnipotent and divine,
Will Thy blessed Son return to earth?
When will heaven's treasures sublime
Be possessed by those of the Second Birth?

When, Lord God and Ruler supreme,
Will Your temporal blessing of time end?
When will hosts from heaven stream
Toward earth with Christ, man's best Friend?

When, Lord God, gracious and kind,
Will Thy mercy with mortal man be past?
When will Satan no longer blind
Those who need to trust the First and Last?

When, Lord God, benefactor of grace,
Will earth's mortals seek Your will and way?
When shall we see our Saviour's face?
When will Christ Jesus His power display?

When, Lord God, eternal paragon of love,
Will Thy justice pervade this earth?
When will mortals with Thy saints above
Praise Thee and Thy Son for their Second Birth?

When, Lord God, epitome of righteousness,
Will Christ Jesus come Thy judgment to bring?
Earth's saints are waiting His coming to bless
And acknowledge Him as Lord and King.

When, Lord God, will all these things be?
When will the spirit of man seek Thy face?
When will the Church to heaven flee
To share forever Thy love and Thy grace?

Is Jesus Christ Your King?

This question to earth's busy mortals
This writer would like to bring:
Are you assured of heaven's portals?
Is Jesus Christ your King?

In this world are many prizes
For which mortal man may seek,
But, Fate holds many surprises
Of which we now would speak.

Do you know you will see tomorrow?
Do you know Him whom God did send?
Do you love the One from whom you borrow
The years of life He is willing to lend?

Do you know God's desire for man?
Have you experienced His mercy and grace?
Have you accepted God's Salvation Plan
By trusting Christ who died in your place?

Are you aware Time is fleeting?
And that soon your choice will be made?
Are you ready for that greeting
That mortal man fain would evade?

Known only to God is that great day
When His Son shall return to this earth;
Until that time man continues his way
Accepting or rejecting his Second Birth.

Some mortals will win victory, others suffer defeat
Determined by the Anchor to which they cling;
The future will be wonderful and sweet
For those souls who trust Christ Jesus as King.

Without Jesus

Without Jesus where would mortals be
As Time's diminishing years unfold?
Only His redeeming blood can free
The "lost" from Satan's stranglehold.

Without Jesus there would be no hope
For mortal man to have immortal life;
Without Jesus man would blindly grope
Helplessly mired in trouble and strife.

Without Jesus there is no real joy
Upon this temporal planet Earth,
For only those trusting Him can enjoy
This life and know its true worth.

Without Jesus Satan's forces would rule,
His demonic servants would hold sway;
Their actions would be ruthless and cruel,
Filling mortals with fear and dismay.

Without Jesus there would be no grace
Bestowed undeservedly upon earth's "lost"
Nor would he prepare a home in space
For those whose trust He paid sin's cost.

Without Jesus there would be no love
Bestowed continually upon earth's mortals,
For Jesus is the love from heaven above
That provides access to heaven's portals.

Without Jesus life would be truly vain,
For man's values are merely dross;
Nothing could cover man's sin stain
Resulting in his soul's eternal loss.

Man's Fateful Choice

When I consider the wondrous glory
Christ renounced to come to earth,
I thank God for the gospel story
And His Plan for man's "second birth."

The wonders of heaven I cannot conceive
Of whose beauty the angels must sing,
But I thank God who gave me faith to believe
In Christ Jesus as Saviour and King.

Heaven's treasures one day I will share
As will all those who trust in God's Son,
For in Judgment each life is laid bare
Revealing those whom salvation have won.

Earth's mortals have perceived God's grace
And are aware of sin's fateful cost;
Soon Eternity temporal Time will replace
And man's chance for salvation will be lost.

God's mercy has let it be known
In His Holy and Eternal Book;
Faith in Christ must be shown,
For another way it's futile to look.

When one contemplates the frailty of man
And Satan's any conquests in the past,
The wise will hasten to accept God's Plan,
Which through Eternity's aeons will last.

The unbeliever, and other servants of sin
Who ignore the warning men speak,
A devil's hell they surely shall win
And face a future unutterably bleak.

Beyond

Beyond the setting sun abides the night,
Beyond the distances telescopes can scan
Are creations of dazzling delight
That Christ is preparing for man.

Beyond mortal man's powers to conceive
Heaven's glories will be his to share;
Rich blessings man will daily receive
Under the Saviour's watch and care.

Beyond the reach of Satan's seductive call,
Beyond the scope of mortal man's mind,
Peace and serenity and justice for all
Earth's true Christians will ultimately find.

Beyond this earth in the reaches of space
The Trinity in indescribable splendor dwell;
Mere words are inadequate to describe the place
And no mortal tongue its magnificence can tell.

Beyond the memory of temporal time
Earth's saved shall be with Christ, God's Son,
For it is by faith in our Saviour divine
That all the benefits of heaven are won.

Beyond Death's veil there eternally abides
Future glories Christ will willingly share;
Yet, now these wondrous blessings God hides
Which later will be Christian's daily fare.

Beyond the reach of Satan, hell and sin,
Eternity offers enchanting rewards to man;
Repentance and faith in Christ Jesus will win,
The Salvation that was and is God's Only Plan.

Where Will You Be?

Where will you be when Time is no more
Than a forgotten memory in the dim past?
Will you be on heaven's glorious shore
With Christ Jesus, the First and Last?

Where will you be as Time's days are spent?
Are this world's treasures precious to you?
Are you too proud your many sins to repent?
Are you content in the vain things you do?

Where will you be when God shall decide
That the hour is near for His Son to return?
Have you given God your life and in Him abide
Or His Way do you continue to spurn?

Where will you be when calamities fall
On the sin-fettered mortals of Earth?
Have you answered God's patient call
Offering mankind the "Second Birth"?

Where will you be when Christ shall return
To reclaim His own from this Earth?
Do you desire that for which mortals yearn
God's gift of greatest worth?

Where will you be when this present earth
Has its last orbit run?
Will you have had your "Second Birth"
Ere Eternity has begun?

Where will you be God wants to know
As His mercy and grace still abide?
The wise their faith in Christ will show
Whose shed blood their sins will hide.

He (Jesus) Came

He came that mortals may have life;
He came to rescue them from strife;
He came when the sin of unbelief was rife;
His own received Him not.

He came from His heavenly home in space;
He came to show God's amazing grace;
He came to die in sinful mankind's place;
His life sin could not blot.

He came to make God's Plan known;
He came so God's mercy might be shown;
He came that Believers Salvation could own
By showing faith in His Holy Name.

He came sin's enticements to fight;
He came to conquer wrong with right;
He came to defeat the Prince of Night
To absolve Believers from sin and shame.

He came to Earth sinless and pure;
He came that mortals Salvation could secure;
He came with redemption which will endure;
He offers Salvation to mortal man.

He came and others His attributes tell;
He came to claim those under Satan's spell;
He came to rescue multitudes from Hell
If by faith they accept God's Plan.

How

How evident the errant nature of man
That leads him down the path of sin;
How gracious is God's Salvation Plan
Which gift believing mortals may win.

How flawless is the Bible, God's Eternal Book
That points mankind toward Christ, His Son;
It proves that Christ is the Saviour for whom we look
And reveals how His victory over sin was won.

How patient God is when dealing with mortals,
Today and tomorrow He is always the same;
His Son is preparing mansions in Heaven's portals
For each Believer who trusts in His Name.

How fateful is mankind's choice during life
When each is allowed his destiny to choose;
Choice must be made prior to Time's reaping knife
Or their precious souls they will lose.

How charitable is our God to provide
Sustenance and protection for Earth's teeming host;
How merciful is the Holy Spirit to guide
Repentant souls to Christ, Whom they need most.

How loving is our God Who this Earth sustains,
How powerful His maintenance of planets in space,
How sufficient is Christ's blood to cover sin's stains
For each true Believer who trusts in His grace.

How tenderhearted is God who wants mortals to be saved
From the penalty of committed sins while on Earth;
How crowded is hell's broad road which is neatly paved
With broken promises of those needing a Second Birth.

Hold On!

Hold on, you hesitant Believers of Earth,
Hold on, Christ Jesus is on your side;
You, who have had the Second Birth,
You, who have become the Saviour's Bride.

Hold on, Time is hastening to his sure end,
Hold on, God knows the troubles you endure,
You, to who Christ is Saviour and Friend,
You, whose promised future is eternally secure.

Hold on, thank God for each precious day,
Hold on, you know that trials come to all,
You, who have trusted Christ Jesus, the Way,
You, who from His refuge never can fall.

Hold on, continue the Holy Bible to believe,
Hold on, Christ Jesus is the Anchor of your soul,
You, whom God has chosen to reprieve,
You, whom Christ's shed blood has made whole.

Hold on, do not let Satan confuse your goal,
Hold on, let your witness for Christ be bold,
You, whose faith must not become a shoal,
You, whose future promises blessings untold.

Hold on, let your witness for Christ be true,
Hold on, let your life be free from fear,
You, should follow Christ's example in all you do,
You, whom our blessed Saviour holds so dear.

Hold on, let nothing sever your service to God,
Hold on, let your conduct be pleasing to his Son,
You, whom life's sojourn on this earth must trod,
You, whose faith in Christ has life's victory won.

There's No Danger There, Near Jesus

Asleep in a ship the "Master" lay,
Peacefully awaiting the coming day;
Though angry waves the ship did sway,
There's no danger there, near Jesus.

The Disciples recognized their plight,
Vainly hoping for morning's light;
Not realizing in their fright
There's no danger there, near Jesus.

The ship was shaken and violently tossed,
The Disciples thought that all was lost;
Afraid this voyage their lives would cost,
There's no danger there, near Jesus.

"Awake, Master, ere we sink and die,"
Arose the chorused pleading cry;
While failing arms the oars did ply,
There's no danger there, near Jesus.

The "Master" did what only He could do;
He calmed the waves and the wind that blew;
The Disciples found these words were true:
There's no danger there, near Jesus.

Unworthy

Unworthy am I of God's gracious care,
Whose home is in Heaven above;
Yet I'm destined to spend eternity there
Because of the "Saviour's" love.

Unworthy am I of God's fathomless grace,
Whose power in the universe we see;
Yet I'm destined to behold His Son's face
Who died that each man might be free.

Unworthy am I of God's wondrous love,
Revealed by the death of His Son;
Yet I'm destined to live with Christ above
And to share in the victory He won.

Unworthy am I of God's goodness shown,
In His provision for rescuing man;
Yet I'm destined to see Christ on His throne
With others who have accepted God's Plan.

Unworthy, unrighteous, unclean and unjust,
A guilty sinner condemned and lost;
Unwilling to show saving faith and trust
In the Christ who paid my sin's cost.

Yet God's great mercy was not spent
And under the Holy Spirit's control,
God gave me faith to believe and repent
And I trusted Christ with my soul.

Worthy am I of Heaven's treasures great,
Since Christ's blood has cleansed my sin;
Won't you trust Christ before it's too late
That Heaven's treasures you too may win?

A Christian's Prayer

Lord, in awe I contemplate Thy power
And marvel at Thy limitless grace;
I await that future glorious hour
When I shall behold Thy face.

Lord, I offer grateful thanks to Thee
For every expression of Thy bountiful love,
For Thy willingness to die for me
And for preparing my eternal home above.

Lord, I thank Thee for each day
And for the earth on which I live;
For these gifts I could not pay,
Hence, my life in Thy service I give.

Lord, those I love; one and all,
Wilt Thou with them Thy blessings share?
May each one heed the Holy Spirit's call
To insure a part of Thy heavenly fare.

Lord, for other dear ones whom I know
Who desperately need Thy saving grace,
I pray to them Your mercy will flow
Till in repentance they seek Your face.

Lord, for those who reject Your call
Who know You paid their sin's cost,
Impress on them the fearful fatal fall
That awaits each soul that's lost.

Lord Jesus, hear this humble prayer of mine
And reveal anew your mercy and grace,
That many may share Your home sublime
In the security of Thy dwelling place.

Time, Time to Choose

Ceaseless as a river flowing,
Silent as the rising moon,
Time rushes by, never slowing,
Forever gone, all too soon.

Priceless as a precious stone
Provided by a heavenly plan,
Time reveals God's love shown
For each weak and sinful man.

Time is limited for each mortal man,
Silently and swiftly does it flee;
Christ finished God's Salvation Plan
That each Believer might be free.

Man's envy brings hate and strife
Over earthly treasures to be won,
Ignoring the gift of eternal life
Found by faith in God's Holy Son.

Time is life, the two are one;
Spent time man cannot regain;
Eternal are the blessings won
By faith in our Saviour's Name.

Time grows short and Death is near,
Mortal man soon must choose;
Christ or Satan, the choice is clear,
Eternal life to win or lose.

Time is a Reaping Knife

I saw an injured moth today
Who by a great effort could fly;
I know not how he came that way
But, I knew he soon would die.

Ere Time had passed an hour,
He lay inert upon his side;
As in obedience to some Power,
He fluttered once then died.

I know not whence he came
Nor why God gave him life,
Yet, he's gone just the same,
For Time is a reaping knife.

I know not how this earth was made
Nor why God loves mortal man,
But, I do know man cannot evade
His duty to accept God's Plan.

In God's Plan Christ Jesus came
To save earth's mortals from sin;
He came to bear each sinner's blame,
So God's gift of Salvation they'd win.

"It is finished!" Christ Jesus cried,
A willing victim of Time's knife,
Dying for all, His own wishes He denied,
Purchasing for others endless life.

Man or moth, each must fall
Before Time's reaping knife;
All who are wise in faith will call
On Christ for eternal life.

The Hand of God

How tightly do you hold His hand,
The hand of God, I mean,
Which leads, guides and protects
And still remains unseen?

Is your hand frail and weak
Whose health and strength has fled
Because you have forgotten God
And you need to be spiritually fed?

Or is the strength of your hand known
To people far and near
By the life you live and witness give
Without any thought of fear?

My hand is weak I must confess;
I wish that it were strong,
So I want God to hold my hand
To keep me where I belong.

God Sustains

Quiet as falling flower seeds
As sure as each day's birth,
God provides for each man's needs
To sustain him on this earth.

God makes the lowly carrots grow
And green peas to fill each pod;
He does this to plainly show
That He is a merciful God.

God makes an apple a burnished red
And another with a golden hue;
By myriad seeds the birds are fed,
For God gives them their due.

God created the rivers that flow
And fish their streams to share;
He made plants in the rivers grow
To provide food for fish welfare.

A pecan tree which towers tall
With branches of fruit for man
Gives up its fruit in early fall
In obedience to a celestial plan.

God causes the refreshing rain to fall
To nourish each herb and flower;
God desires that man on Him shall call
And shall praise Him for His power.

Our gracious God does this earth sustain,
His love is its suspension cord:
He wants man from evil to abstain
And show faith in Christ the Lord.

God's Plan

When I ponder the ages now past
And contemplate the future of man,
I think of Christ, the First and Last
And how He completed God's Plan.

Every mortal's time on this temporal earth
Like a vapor will fade fast away;
Each mortal's actions and their true worth
Will be revealed on Judgment Day.

Mankind now is faced with a choice:
In life there are two paths to tread;
Each mortal hears his master's voice
And by his spirit is fatefully led.

This question now I'd like to pose,
Which eternal master do you choose?
Ere in death your eyes do close
Your eternal soul you'll save or lose.

Christ Jesus, God's Holy Son,
Is my choice and I hope yours too,
For by faith in Him is won
Heaven's treasures which are ever new.

Those who heed Satan's tempting voice
Who serve him and follow his way
Will too late know their wrong choice
And their doom on Judgment Day.

This statement is true I hasten to say
Concerning the future of man;
The wise shall rejoice; the foolish pay
For their actions concerning God's Plan.

The Calvary Cross

The Calvary Cross was a cruel thing
But our Saviour had no fear;
Sinless He came, Salvation to bring
To those who are willing to hear.

The cross He carried for you and me
Was God's just punishment for sin
And His triumphant death on that tree
Was the battle He alone could win.

'Neath the heavy cross and the sins of the world,
He fell as He approached the hill,
Unmindful of reproach and rebuke at Him hurled,
Thinking only of His Father's will.

There came to His aid a strong, stalwart man
Upon whom was laid the cross
And he carried this load to aid in God's Plan
Of saving men from eternal loss.

On the top of the hill our Saviour died
With a prayer on His lips for man:
"Father, forgive them," He earnestly cried
As He finished the "Salvation Plan."

God in mercy has provided the Way,
By His Son's death on the tree;
Repent of your sin, confess Him today
And receive His Salvation so free.

The Rose

Long have I admired the rose
With its colors rich and rare,
Which, till Time its petals close
Its beauty it delights to share.

From morn till sun has set
Its fragrance mild and sweet
Fills each admirer with regret
They did not sooner meet.

High its lovely head is raised
As it reaches toward the sky,
For the rose our God is praised
Since its beauty none can deny.

Like man, the brilliant rose depends
Upon God for sun and rain
And from each shower that God sends,
The rose will new beauty gain.

Soon the beautiful rose will fade,
Its reign's end will Time disclose;
This ordained fate it cannot evade
And silently its petals will close.

The rose is not dead, merely sleeps
As an open illustration to man
That all of Nature obediently seeks
To be true to God's heavenly plan.

In the spring God will again raise
Another rose like the one we knew
That mortal man again may praise
The gracious God of Creation anew.

A Prayer

Lord Jesus, omnipotent and divine,
May Thy celestial ways be mine;
Fill my heart with renewed love
For Thee and Thy kingdom above.

Lord Jesus, wilt Thou in mercy impart
Faith and strength to my faint heart;
Lord, I also ask Thee my life to lead
And for Thy continuing blessings I plead.

Lord Jesus, wilt Thou this prayer hear:
Grant salvation to those I hold dear,
These who Satan has securely caught
Lest their lives be lived for naught.

Lord Jesus, Satan has great power,
He is winning many battles this hour;
May Thy love and mercy hold sway
And may Thy will be done each day.

Lord Jesus, I pray that Your grace
My selfish acts and desires replace;
I pray for knowledge that I might win
Many lost souls who now delight in sin.

Lord Jesus, Thy divinity I again confess
And ask that Thou my witness bless;
Lord, those whom Satan causes to wait
Help me to them Your warning relate.

Lord Jesus, as surely as Satan's coming defeat,
Those trusting in You will savor sweet
The blessings given by the Father and Son
To those whose faith heaven's prize has won.

In Nature Autumn Speaks

Among Autumn's scenes of splendor
Stand trees with leaves of gold,
And my heart is filled with wonder
While their beauty I behold.

Nature prepares trees for winter's chill
By removing their golden leaves,
Making barren branches, mute and still,
Impervious to each frigid breeze.

"I am not dead, I merely sleep,"
Each somber giant seems to say;
"Every year this rendezvous I keep
While winter's winds hold sway."

"When spring arrives and I awake,
On God's bounty again to feed;
From fertile earth I daily take
All the nourishment that I need."

May we, like a flourishing tree so green,
Trust the Creator with our lives;
Placing our faith in Him, who remains unseen,
Whose power we see in azure skies.

If Christ in Nature each tree sustain,
Providing for each changing hour;
He will save all who trust in His Name
By His matchless, eternal power.

Calvary

Calvary, what a poignant name,
Scene of suffering, sin and shame;
Where the Saviour took our blame,
When on the cross He died.

Calvary, that truly desolate place,
Where the Saviour hung in space;
And God in mercy turned His face,
While His Son was crucified.

Calvary, that barren, gloomy hill,
Where Christ His destiny did fulfill;
And death His plaintive cry did still,
Christ Jesus, God's Holy Son.

Calvary, sin and death were defeated here,
Though few believers were standing near;
For the others had fled in fear,
While Christ His victory won.

Calvary, where flowed a crimson tide,
From the Saviour's head and side;
Given in payment for His Bride,
Who serve Him in grateful love.

Calvary, once again the Saviour will see,
When all who lived will bow the knee;
And Christ will take all He has made free
To share Heaven's mansions above.

Responsibility to Our Jesus
(An Acrostic Poem)

Renew my faith, revive my heart,
Each day is my earnest prayer;
Search my soul to its inmost part,
Place a compassion for others there.

Once a sinner condemned and lost,
Now a servant of the King;
Since Christ has paid my sin's cost
I am happy His praises to sing.

But Christ expects more than praising song
In grateful service from His own,
Let each Christian be faithful and strong
In witnessing of the mercy Christ has shown.

Tell of Christ's love, His matchless grace,
Yes, speak of His death on the cross;
Trust Him for Salvation and seek His face
Or face your soul's inevitable loss.

Only Christ Jesus can save from sin,
Unite with Him that you may stand;
Rewards in Heaven you'll surely win,
Joining His joyous Heavenly band.

Each day you reject Christ's pleading call,
Satan comes closer to owning your soul,
Union with Christ will prevent your fall
Since He alone can make you whole.

Tomorrow

Tomorrow is a word mortals freely use;
Its employment is increasingly slanted;
Countless are those whom their souls lose
Because tomorrow was taken for granted.

Today is a tomorrow mortals looked for,
I wonder what its precious hours brought;
Is mankind aware what the future has in store
For those in whom Satan's net are caught?

Lost souls are those who have yet to believe
On Christ Jesus as Saviour and King;
Unless they trust Him they cannot receive
The Salvation that He died to bring.

Many unsaved look for a tomorrow
When they plan to trust Christ for Salvation;
Such procrastination portends great sorrow
Regardless of one's rank or station.

Tomorrow is the gift only God can give
And by mortals it may be lost or won;
The Bible reveals how mortals should live
And that Salvation is found in God's Son.

Tomorrow if received grants mortals more time,
Time, their soul's destiny to insure;
Blessed will be those trusting our Saviour Divine
Whose redemption will forever endure.

Past history this great truth does relate,
Judgment on mankind God has ordained;
Only true Believers will enter heaven's gate,
All others in Hell's darkness are eternally chained.

Christ Jesus Passed This Way

Before God had created Time
From the realm of eternal day,
According to His will divine
Christ Jesus passed this way.

Christ Jesus made the light
That changes the night to day;
All stars were formed by His might,
As Creator He passed this way.

In great mercy and grace sublime,
God formed mortal man from clay,
Gave him a soul and temporal time,
For Christ Jesus would pass this way.

The weak mortals that God made
Let evil in their lives hold sway,
Yet, sin's penalty they can evade
Since Christ Jesus passed this way.

On earth Christ lived a perfect life
And He willingly died to pay
The penalty for man's sin and strife
As Saviour Christ passed this way.

The Saviour broke death's sure hold
To Satan and his follower's dismay
And God offers man His riches untold
Since Christ Jesus passed this way.

From Heaven God offers His hand
To those trusting Christ to pay
Their fare to that celestial land
Since faith in Christ is the only way.

Beyond

Beyond the vision of mortal man
Hidden by the black veil of space;
Beyond even the Sun's piercing span
Resides an eternal abode of grace.

Beyond the knowledge of mortal man,
Beyond his power to think or reason,
God conceived His "Salvation Plan"
And offers it to man for a season.

Beyond these days of extended grace,
Beyond the years that come and go,
God resides in His dwelling place
And to mortals His blessing flow.

Beyond the hour Time shall end
When endless Eternity holds sway;
Additional years God will not lend
Nor will He man's judgment delay.

Beyond God's proffered grace
And far from heaven's eternal day,
There is another dwelling place
Where the "lost" forever must stay.

Beyond the reach of God's hand,
Beyond the help of angels above,
The "lost" of Earth forever stand
For having rejected Christ's love.

Beyond the bounds of heaven's light,
Beyond the reach of comfort and aid,
Chained by the darkness of hell's night,
There, sin's dread penalty is paid.

One Day

One day this imperfect body of mine
Will be changed in the twinkling of an eye,
Fashioned after our Saviour Divine
Who will be seen returning in the sky.

My feet will know no aches nor pains
Since Time's bridge to Eternity has been spanned
And I shall travel to celestial domains
In accordance as our Saviour has planned

My fading eyes will no longer be dim
And the strength of my arms will be vast;
My body will be perfect when I see Him
As mortal restraints are a thing of the past.

My new voice shall joyously sing to our Lord
With sound and tone pleasant to hear;
Heaven's host jubilantly will take up the chord
With adoring voices sounding loud and clear.

My hands, now strong and sure, I'll raise
Toward our approaching Saviour in the sky;
My lips with the countless host will praise
God's Perfect Lamb who was willing to die.

My ears will hear the sweetest sound
A voice only the saved can hear;
"Come to where eternal blessings abound
To a land without violence and fear."

My heart will pound as never before
And my joy will increase and o'erflow
When with the host I reach that shore
Where God's eternal blessings we'll know.

Beyond Belief

Beyond belief is man's inhumanity to man,
Beyond belief that God still cares for the human race,
Beyond belief that God still offers His Plan
Of Salvation for those trusting Jesus died in their place.

Beyond belief is the undeniable fact
That Earth's mortals ignore our Creator above;
Beyond belief is the penalty God will exact
Of those who refuse His offer of love.

Beyond belief is the ignorance of mortals
Whose carnal desires their nature reveals;
Beyond belief is the suffering behind Hell's portals
From which place is no relief or appeals.

Beyond belief is man's wanton waste of time,
A waste of time that he can ill afford;
Beyond belief are the celestial rewards sublime
For those who trust Christ Jesus as Lord.

Beyond belief that man should forget God's power,
Beyond belief that God's miracles are not believed,
Yet, each doomed doubter will experience the hour
When he wishes on Christ Jesus he had believed.

Beyond belief is the future in store
For those failing in Jesus to trust,
For our Saviour in truth is Heaven's Door
And for Salvation trusting Him is a must.

Beyond belief is what spiritual apathy brings,
Beyond belief that Time's duration has been set,
Yet, believing mortals to God's promises cling
And in Heaven their every need will be met.

Waiting

Upon this unique planet called Earth
Mortals wait while Time races by;
Some seek the precious Second Birth
While others its reality deny.

Some wait for Fortune on them to smile,
Some wait for conditions to improve;
Many are those whom Satan does beguile
The weakness of humanity to prove.

Waiting and enjoying God's blessings on man,
Waiting and engrossed in worldly pleasures,
Waiting and still indifferent about God's Plan,
Which if accepted brings unspeakable treasures.

Waiting, while God's preachers proclaim
That Earth's mortals their sins should repent,
Waiting and rejecting God's Lamb slain
Who was and is the only Saviour God sent.

Waiting for what the future will bring,
Waiting and hoping that tomorrow will be better,
Waiting for something to which to cling,
Waiting, willingly held in Satan's strong fetter.

Waiting, for something they know not what,
Waiting, wishing, wanting and wondering,
Waiting, under the cloud of sin's dark blot
While Time their years is plundering.

Waiting, for a future doubt will have won
Unless they turn from their sin and repent
And show faith in Christ Jesus, God's Holy Son
Ere their lives' last hour has been spent.

Trust Me

Trust Me, our Saviour said,
I am the Truth, the Way;
I have risen from the dead,
My death for your sin did pay.

Trust Me in your journey through life,
When troubles your soul do press:
I can help you overcome any strife
And am willing your life to bless.

Trust Me while many others forget Me
And seem to live in their own world;
Faith in Me will from sin set you free,
Let faith like a banner be unfurled.

Trust Me because I am your Friend;
I want what is best for you;
Upon My help you can surely depend,
For my nature is steadfast and true.

Trust Me when you have a need
Or a problem that must be met,
For you I suffered and did bleed;
May My sacrifice you not forget.

Trust Me when life's threatening perils abound,
My mercy and grace are still offered to all;
Salvation in My Name by faith is found,
I will answer each Believer's trusting call.

Trust Me, for mankind's time will soon end,
Bringing Judgment to the mortals of Earth;
The Holy Bible reveals that God will send
Me to receive those who have had a Second Birth.

O Time

O Time, invaluable gift from God above
Whose blessings to mankind defy number,
You are the continuing expression of God's love
While mortals appear deep in slumber.

O Time, when will mankind ever awake
To the incalculable worth of thy days?
When, O Time, will evil they forsake
To escape the penalty of their ways?

O Time, does not mankind yet know
The Salvation Plan our God conceived?
Why are Earth's mortals hesitant to show
That God's only Salvation Plan is believed?

O Time, thy passing brings nearer the day
That our Saviour shall return for His own:
God desires mortals their faith to display
In Christ, whose love on the cross was shown.

O Time, convey this message to the "lost"
Who ignore God and His warnings to man;
Eternity in hell will be the dread cost
Awaiting those rejecting God's benevolent plan.

O Time, when thy gift to mankind is complete
And Eternity will hold full sway,
Believers in Christ in communion sweet
Will enjoy Heaven's endless day.

O Time, while your hours yet abide,
Bear this final warning to those who doubt;
From sin's penalty no sinner can hide,
Redemption is reserved for Believers devout.

Although

Although my mind cannot conceive
The omnipotent power of our God,
With my heart and soul I do believe
He created Earth's mortals from sod.

Although my eyes view azure skies
And their being I cannot comprehend,
Their size and scope mortal reason defies
While their beauty they continue to lend.

Although this planet Earth continues to turn
In accordance with Gods Celestial Plan,
I do not know why mortals continue to spurn
God's gracious Redemption Plan.

Although I know the mighty Sun's rays
Sustain life on this planet called Earth,
I believe God detests man's sinful ways
Desiring each to have a Second Birth.

Although mankind still seems unconcerned
About the swift passage of Time,
Eternal will be the penalty for God's love spurned
And failure to trust in our Saviour divine.

Although mortal life on this planet Earth
Still continues because of God's love,
I believe only those with a Second Birth
Will inherit Heaven's mansions above.

Although the future mortals cannot know,
For this power God alone does possess,
By these few words I'd like to show
That each true Believer God will bless.

Alone

Alone our wonderful Saviour came
To live on this planet called Earth,
Leaving in Heaven His glory and fame,
Condescending to a mere mortal's birth.

Alone He left His Father's side
To live and die for mankind's sin;
Had He chosen in Heaven to abide,
There would be no salvation to win.

Alone on the cross He endured the pain
For mankind whom sin had depraved,
Knowing His sacrifice was not in vain,
For through it many mortals would be saved.

Alone He was buried in a follower's grave,
Tenderly borne there by grieving Saints
Who in sorrow forgot He came to save
And that He would overcome mortal restraints.

The grave was no match for God's Holy Son
Who arose His destiny to fulfill,
Proving to mankind that Salvation could be won,
Doubting tongues to shame and still.

Alone Christ returned to His Father above
To receive eternal honor, praise and glory;
Successfully He demonstrated God's great love
And His life on Earth is the Gospel Story.

Alone Christ came to become The Way
To prevent mankind from being eternally lost;
In Heaven He will rule the endless day
Since He was willing to pay its fearful cost.

Our God, the Great I Am

Among the enigmas facing the human race
Beyond the comprehension of mortal man
Hidden within the limitless reaches of space,
Resides our God, the great I Am.

Although unseen by any mortal eye,
Almighty God is supreme, eternal;
His countless creations which description defy
Are the fruition of a Plan Supernal.

The mysterious, magnificent creations in space,
Our God's omnipotence tells;
Yet, His creation of the mortal human race
All other creation excels.

The innumerable gigantic spheres in space
Reveal their beauty in darkest night,
Invisibly anchored in a predestined place,
Their timeless beauty an awesome sight.

These countless creations reveal to man
Our Creator's ability to achieve,
Yet, these creations are dwarfed by His Plan
For mortals Salvation to receive.

From Heaven's realms of eternal glory,
God the Father sent His Holy Son
Whose life on Earth is the Gospel Story,
Revealing how Salvation is won.

Now, in Heaven, our God patiently waits
for mankind on His Son to believe;
Salvation is in Christ Jesus the Bible relates
Available for true Believers to receive.

What Mortals Should Know

I do not know what the future holds
Nor what tomorrow will bring,
But, I do know as Time quietly unfolds
My trust is in Christ our King.

I do not know when this planet Earth
Will meet its predestined end,
But, I do know of the Second Birth
Found in Christ Jesus our Friend.

I do not know why trials come
To Earth's Christians one and all,
But, I do know their total sum
Christ will bear lest we fall.

I do not know why mortals should live
As if they were the masters of Earth,
For Time and Life are God's to give;
A mortal's faith determines their worth.

I do know what mortals should fear,
For sin's bands only Christ can sever
And the Bible makes this abundantly clear;
Christ Jesus as King will reign forever.

I do know that each mortal must face
God's judgment at his life's inevitable end
And blessed are those who accept His grace
By trusting Christ as Saviour and Friend.

I do know that Salvation is won
By repentant souls trusting in Christ's Name,
For God has decreed faith in His Son
Will suffice for man's sin and shame.

I do know when Time is no more
And this Earth is mere cosmic dust,
All who reside on Heaven's shore
Will be those who in Jesus did trust.

Could I?

Could Heaven's glories I recite,
Describe its scenes of utter delight,
Within your heart would there ignite
A love of God others have known?

None can describe Heaven's jeweled wall
Or convey the splendor of a golden hall;
This beautiful home from which none can fall
Where God's love for mankind is shown.

Could I explain why the Saviour came,
How He died at Calvary for man's blame,
Would you live your life just the same?
Would you reject our blessed Lord?

The Holy Bible reveals how Christ arose
Defeating Death and satanic foes;
God's boundless mercy and love to disclose,
Which hold mankind as a strong cord.

May I speak of a Judgment Day
When Christ Jesus will hold sway,
The hour when all mankind shall pay
For each sinful act and deed.

May I hasten to reveal
Man's sin he cannot conceal
Nor its penalty can he repeal
In his greatest hour of need.

But, thanks to God there is a way
To Heaven's eternal realms of day
For repentant souls who will display
Their faith in Christ Jesus, God's Son.

The wise will not this chance refuse
Lest eternal life they surely lose
But, as Spirit-led by faith they choose
Christ Jesus, their salvation is won.

God's Plan, Completed

God caused the golden Sun to shine;
He placed clouds in a sky of blue;
The planets reveal His Hand Divine
That made each creation new.

The stars were fashioned and hung in space
And their orbits were celestially ordained;
Each creation reveals true artistic grace
And the Power by which it's sustained.

This Earth too by His Hand was wrought
As was the Moon in space above;
To this temporal home man was brought
That he might worship a God of love.

Weak mankind soon fell a victim of sin,
For Satan was quick to beguile;
Yet, God made provision so man could win
Salvation, that makes life worthwhile.

Prophets and Apostles came with God's Word
And His Plan did they patiently reveal;
Repentance and Faith were themes men heard
If their sins they desired to conceal.

Christ Jesus, our Lord, God's Holy Son
Shed His blood to cover sin's blame;
Eternal Salvation may only be won,
By faith shown in His Holy Name.

Jesus, our Saviour, Who died for the lost
Is in Heaven now preparing a place;
Faith in Him alone pays the admission cost
To win this home of perpetual grace.

Lord God

Lord God, I acknowledge Thy great power,
Thy love for the needy human race;
Thy mercy falls as an endless shower
Intermingled with Thy infinite grace.

Lord God, Thy strength I sorely need;
Lead me with Thy strong hand;
Help me daily on Thy Word to feed
And for Thy cause to bravely stand.

Lord God, guide Thou my errant feet
And light the dark paths that I tread;
Be Thou near lest Satan I meet
And his beguiling ways turn my head.

Lord God, these finite eyes of mine
Drink in the beauty of Thy creation
Made in perfection by Thy Son Divine
As a perpetual witness to every nation.

Lord God, grant my lips shall only speak
To bring honor to thy Name;
Strengthen my spirit lest I become weak
And play Satan's sinful game.

Lord God, grant me wisdom that I may show
Lost souls that they need Salvation today;
Grant they our Saviour will come to know
And in His service soon find their way.

Lord God, before Time his last our does spend,
May those lost souls whom we love
Trust Christ Jesus as Saviour and Friend,
Thus inheriting a celestial home above.

If

If your composure you can retrain
While others are trying in vain,
If false blame is laid at your door,
Do you remain as calm as before?

In yourself do you continue to trust
When others say that you're unjust?
If you're condemned by many a voice,
Do you uphold their freedom of choice?

If you can wait and your vigor retain
Be lied about and your tongue refrain,
If others make you the object of hate,
Do you decline their act to berate?

Can you refrain from appearing too good
And talking more wisely than you should?
If you can dream and reject their hold,
If you can think and have thoughts unfold.

Can you meet triumph and fame
And ill-fated disaster the same?
If your truth to fool others is bent,
Do you to vain indignation give vent?

If the best of your achievements suffer defeat,
Do you rebuild though your tools are effete?
If your total winnings are wagered and lost,
Do you start again, not mentioning the cost?

If your heart, your sinew and nerve
Are failing, yet continuing to serve,
If within sees empty and vain,
Does the will to "hold on" remain?

If you can converse with crowds and be true,
Walk with kings and be the friend common people knew,
If neither foes nor loving friends can offend,
Yet, help toward their goals you would lend.

If each minute you can fully spend
And God's service into its seconds blend,
Yours is the Earth and Salvation is won
By faith shown in Christ, God's Holy Son.

Jesus Is Our Saviour's Name

There is a Name, I love to hear,
The Name heaven's hosts in adoration sing,
A Name that dispels doubt and fear,
Jesus, our blessed, eternal King.

Yes, Jesus is the peerless Name
To whose cause mortals should cling,
For in great mercy Jesus came
God's Gift of salvation to bring.

When it seemed that all was lost,
Jesus came from heaven's glory;
He simply came to pay sin's cost,
Which is the eternal Gospel Story.

Jesus lived upon this Earth;
His life from sin was free;
He offers mortals the Second Birth;
He heeds each earnest plea.

God's Plan for Redemption He will not alter,
For Salvation's cruel cost has been paid;
Jesus in God's purpose did not falter
Nor by His sufferings was He dismayed.

Some mortals seek peace, searching in vain
In this world of hatred and strife;
They completely ignore God's Lamb slain
Who is the Key to eternal life.

God is patient and God is Just;
He lets mortals choose their own fate;
He sent Jesus for mortals to trust
Before it was eternally too late.

His sin a mortal cannot justify
Nor its dread cost can he pay;
Death's sure call he cannot defy
If his name is called some day.

The lost who are wise will fall on their face
And pray for God's Spirit to come in;
Jesus will answer with mercy and grace
And will save each confessor from his sin.

Indescribable

I cannot conceive a more beautiful face
Than yours in the picture before me;
I cannot imagine the attendant grace
Of the vision of enchantment I see.

I bask in the beauty so apparent to all,
I revel in the charm of your smile;
I am aware your picture tends to enthrall
And your pulchritude its viewers does beguile.

I enjoy the atmosphere your picture creates
And its is proudly displayed on a shelf;
Its equal couldn't be found in a thousand states,
So this lovely jewel I keep for myself.

Words are inept when they try to reveal
An intriguing loveliness such as your own;
They utterly fail to describe the appeal
Of the dream in the picture that's shown.

Why does the writer attempt to relate
The fascination your picture inspires?
Why is your enchantment beyond debate
And a scene of which one never tires?

Why did our Creator this masterpiece make?
Why did He create this paragon so fair?
He did it so searching mortals could take
Pride in viewing elegance beyond compare.

There are no words the writer can find
That your picture's true beauty can portray;
He thanks our Creator that he is not blind
And daily enjoys this unequaled display.

Man Chooses His Destiny

Multitudes in this world seek glory
And God's Plan they openly disdain,
Turning deaf ears to the Gospel Story,
They choose in their sin to remain.

Our sovereign God patiently waits
In Heaven's bright mansions above;
Though mortal man's sin He hates,
It does not diminish His love.

Time can be man's enemy or friend;
God lends it to those on this Earth;
God in mercy a Saviour did send
To offer each sinner the New Birth.

If man uses Time well and the Saviour finds,
To him it is truly a friend;
If man wastes Time in sin that binds,
To him how bitter its end.

God's will for man is not concealed;
He desires that all mortals shall heed
The Salvation Plan that Christ revealed,
Which each living mortal does need.

As Time continues his constant flight
While this Earth continues to turn,
God offers each mortal endless delight,
Which only the foolish will spurn.

In Heaven's mansions a record is kept,
A record of every thought and deed
While man is being relentlessly swept
Toward the Judgment God has decreed.

God is not willing to use force
To see man's Salvation is won;
Hell shall witness the vain remorse
Of all who reject God's Son.

God's Word to the Lost

There are those who scoff and say
There is no God alive today;
These who foolishly raise their voice
Are making a dreadful fatal choice.

Some men laugh and others scold,
Where is the ancient God of old?
Let us now behold the face
Of Him who created the human race.

To those whom Satan securely holds,
God's Will and Way soon unfolds
And their future is one to dread
Since they are the spiritual dead.

God is eternal, He cannot die,
Though His existence man may deny;
Heaven's creations hung in space
Reveal our God the epitome of grace.

The Earth in quiet splendor reveals
A sample of beauty that Heaven conceals
And though difficult for men to conceive
These glories are there for man to receive.

Time will not wait nor slow his pace
For the doomed of the human race;
Satan will reap the mortals of Earth
Excepting those of the Second Birth.

These words of warning to the lost,
Christ paid for you a fearful cost;
The wise from Satan's camp will flee
To Christ alone Who makes men free.

To the Lost Who Continue to Wait

This poem a message shall bring
Of Christ our Redeemer and King,
The One to Whom man must cling
For life beyond the grave.

Christ Jesus, God's Holy Son
Has life's greatest victory won;
In God's mercy the act was done
That gave Him power to save.

Christ Jesus for man's sin has died;
On Calvary's cross He was crucified,
Suffering death for His Chosen Bride,
Then He arose by His great power.

God has given mortal life to me and you;
Soon its short years will be through;
Then what shall we be able to do
In that final inevitable hour?

When Death comes and we face
The end of this life's fateful race,
Will our inheritance be one of grace
That Christ for us unfolds?

Death shall come however we try
His temporal victory to deny,
For mortals cannot his goals defy
Since God his power upholds.

Now, our God has a definite plan
For this Earth's weak, sinful man
And has given him a life to span
From Time to Eternity.

Now, ere our life's span is spent,
Let's pray to God and our sin repent;
Let's show faith in the Christ God sent
And accept God's serenity.

To the foolish lost who desire to wait,
You face an unbelievably terrible fate,
Which in Eternity's aeons you will hate,
For in hell's domain there is no relief.

May I this final warning repeat?
Christ the Saviour we all shall meet;
The saved shall have communion sweet,
The lost face a fate beyond belief.

A Choice

Upon this spinning planet in space
Omnipotent God placed weak mortal man
Whose daily life depends upon God's grace
And who should seek God's Will and Plan.

Yet, when one travels through the years
That a loving God is pleased to bestow,
One is cognizant of the trouble and tears
Which rampant sin still causes to flow.

It seems that mortals desire to exclude
Thoughts of God from their preoccupied minds;
Few there are who prayer and service include,
Most are enmeshed in Satan's net that binds.

While many a mortal seeks temporal delights
Or is engrossed in a search for power,
God's Will and Way he ignores or slights
Unmindful of a coming Judgment Hour.

God's Holy Bible so clearly reveals
Mortals should seek salvation before Jesus arrives;
They should be aware that Time steals
Their years, their months, their days, their lives.

Almighty God has definitely set the time
When Christ Jesus shall return from heaven above
Who promises rewards, rich and sublime
For repentant Believers who serve Him with love.

In a predestined hour, Time loses his race;
Then will cease God's tender, warning voice;
Eternity for the lost will be in a fearful place
Forever to remember they were given a choice.

Eternal Is Our God

When one's best made plans go astray
Filling Christians with doubt and dismay,
It's only Satan having a field day,
Eternal is our God.

When surrounded by uncertainty and fear
And the future seems dark and drear,
Through Christ the pathway becomes clear,
Eternal is our God.

When others seem to have more than their share
And you only enjoy a very meager fare,
Remember, Christ for His own really does care,
Eternal is our God.

When you contemplate God's plan for your life
While you are surrounded by turmoil and strife
And moral dissolution is increasingly rife,
Eternal is our God.

When mortal goals seem out of reason
When some mortals commit spiritual treason,
Satan is enjoying a late bountiful season,
Eternal is our God.

If Bible promises you may sometimes doubt,
Remember what a Christian's life is about;
God expects Christians to be true and devout,
Eternal is our God.

When Justice seems just a word we hear,
Remember God can calm all doubt and fear;
Let's pray His Son's return is drawing near,
Eternal is our God.

When I Look in the Mirror

When I look in the mirror, what do I see?
I see a total stranger looking back at me;
Gone is the bloom and freshness of youth,
The vision before me sees a bit uncouth.

As I look in the mirror, I remember years past,
I should have considered those times would not last;
Yet, the dilemma I faced was common to all,
Time is unyielding; in his embrace many fall.

Yet, the ancient vision in the mirror I see
Is a true Believer whom Christ Jesus did free;
Buffeted by Time and Satan's blandishments impure,
By faith in Christ Jesus his future is secure.

Now, the vision in the mirror that I see
Would to the lost repeat this warning plea;
To remain an unbeliever you cannot afford,
Trust Christ as Saviour, make Him your Lord.

For there is coming a time and an event
For which Christ Jesus was originally sent;
Jesus came by God's mercy to redeem Earth's lost,
On Calvary's rugged tree, He paid mankind's sin cost.

Soon, there will be seen in God's limitless sky,
Christ and a host man's imagination to defy;
Yet, Christ at this time will not stay on Earth,
He is coming to claim those of the Second Birth.

When the redeemed with Christ ascend on high,
Then the years of Tribulation are truly nigh;
Those left on this Earth this menace must face,
For Satan all righteousness with sin will replace.

In Jesus' Name

In Jesus' Name, omnipotent God,
May Thy blessings upon us fall;
As beings made from Earth's sod
We for Thy mercy now earnestly call.

In this world where Christ is not King
And Satan daily wields his power,
We, as Christians, to Thy promises cling
Which are sufficient for each hour.

Although in this world unbelievers abide
And their power and suppression is shown,
They will be among those trying to hide
When the final days of Tribulation are known.

Lord God, we Thy children praise Thy Name,
We thank Thee for Jesus, Thy Precious Son
Who, to ransom Earth's Believers willingly came
That Salvation in His Name could be won.

Lord God, we need Thy help each day;
As mortals we face many trying hours;
We pray toward us You will grace display
As a merciful revelation of Your powers.

In Jesus' Name our prayers are sent,
For He is the Saviour whom Thou didst provide;
We thank Thee for the years Thou hast lent
And for the Holy Spirit who with us does abide.

In Jesus' Name may our faith not wane
And our lives in Thy service be spent;
Help us show the lost their lives are vain
Until they trust Christ and their sin repent.

For What Goal Do You Seek?

For what goal do you seek?
Is the Master's question to all.
Is your future sure or bleak?
Have you answered the Spirit's call?

In life is your quest for power?
Or are riches your fervent desire?
Are you prepared for that hour
When God's Judgment shall transpire?

Is your life shallow and vain?
Are you proud of what you do?
Is your sin covered or does its stain
Withhold God's blessings from you?

Are you aware of the late hour
And the swift passage of time?
Will you be with those who cower
When confronted by our Saviour Divine?

Do you know that our God is Love?
His Plan for mortals is the best;
Christ is preparing a home above
For those who pass life's test.

Those souls who are not content
With temporal prizes found on Earth
Should, ere their time is spent
Trust Christ for their Second Birth.

Our Saviour has a home prepared
For those who wisely use this hour;
This heavenly home will be shared
By those Christ has saved by His Power.

Time Today, Eternity Tomorrow

When Time has lost his temporal race,
The race he was bound to lose,
Then Earth's mortals shall surely face
The future each was free to choose.

God's grace at this moment shall end
And His mercy shall be no more;
God's message He will no longer send
That Christ Jesus is Heaven's Door.

Man's time for decision will be past
And his future he cannot evade;
His fateful choice forever will last
As will the memory when made.

Today, God's grace freely flows
And Time is still extended to man,
Yet, God is the only One who knows
The final hour of His Redemption Plan.

The earthy treasures that mortals desire
Time will eventually turn to dust,
Yet, the greatest treasure man can acquire
Is simply won by faith and trust.

Each mortal who acknowledges his sin
Believing that Christ Jesus is God's Son
Can by a faith demonstration win
The greatest treasure that can be won.

For this is the aim of God's Plan;
That Earth's mortals should seek His Way,
And God grants Salvation to each man
Who shows faith in Christ in open display.

Is Your Future Secure?

Where were you when Time was born
And Eternity was given its name?
Who witnessed Time's first morn
And who makes each one the same?

Who created your spirit and soul
And how long will they endure?
Who from sin can make you whole
And offers a future that is secure?

God made Time and Eternity too
And by His Will they still abide;
He makes each morn the same, yet new
And your spirit and soul He supplied.

God will make your future secure
If your faith is placed in His Son;
Longer than this earth shall endure
Is eternal life waiting to be won.

Omniscient God knew mortal man would sin
Before Christ created this earth;
He planned that man by faith could win
The gift of the Second Birth.

God's Plan of redemption is complete
Purchased by our Saviour at great cost;
Sin, Hell and Death did Jesus defeat
That man's future might not be lost.

Now, God awaits the decision of man
How he will treat life's greatest prize;
Faith in Christ will complete God's Plan
Securing the future of those who are wise.

When?

When, Lord God, will Christ Thy Son return
As Thou hast promised in Thy Word?
For His appearing Thy saints now yearn
And their pleadings by Thee are heard.

When, Lord God, shall we see His face
Which will set the sky aglow?
When will we experience Thy ultimate grace
That only true Believers will know?

When, Lord God, will Christ extend His hand
As the signal for His saints to rise?
To come and join His heavenly band
In that epoch journey through the skies.

When, Lord God, will we reach that place
Which words are inadequate to describe?
Where, among the limitless realms of space
Does Thy eternal kingdom abide?

When, Lord God, will Thy Son judge man
For the deeds of mortal life?
Bringing Justice according to Thy Plan
Terminating persecution and strife?

When, Lord God, will Judgment be o'er
For Satan and his host so depraved?
When shall we see what is in store
For those whom Thy Son has saved?

Surely, Lord God, our joy will overflow
When our eternal rewards we shall see
And Eternity's aeons will continually show
Thy rich blessings on those who love Thee.

Fate, Man's Free Choice

There is no God, the fool has said;
With these words his fate was sealed;
He joined the host of spiritual dead
Awaiting punishment to be revealed.

I'll think about Christ some other time,
The drunkard was heard to say,
Ignoring the fact that God's Son Divine
Had died man's sin penalty to pay.

The doubter said he didn't believe
That Christ his salvation had won;
God has decreed there is no reprieve
For those who reject His Son.

The procrastinator said some future day
He would consider God's Plan for man;
As long as he lives under Satan's sway
He will have no desire for God's Plan.

The thief is so engrossed in selfish desires
That he forgets eternal life must be won,
Unaware that God's righteousness requires
Mortals repent of sin and show faith in His Son.

The idolater has many gods that he serves;
His life is spent in the worship of things;
Judgment Day will bring what he deserves
As the gods are destroyed to which he clings.

The wise man rejoices and looks ahead;
His future holds no terror or dismay;
His faith is in Christ and Spirit-led,
He will inherit Heaven's eternal day.

God's Plan

When I ponder the ages now past
And contemplate the future of man,
I think of Christ, the First and Last
And how He completed God's Plan.

Every mortal's time on this temporal earth
Like a vapor will fade fast away;
Each man's actions and their true worth
Will be revealed on Judgment Day.

Mankind now is faced with a choice:
In life there are two paths to tread;
Each mortal hears his master's voice
And by his spirit is fatefully led.

This question now I'd like to pose:
Which eternal master do you choose?
Ere in Death your eyes you close,
Your eternal soul you'll save or lose.

Christ Jesus, God's Holy Son,
Is my choice and I hope yours too,
For by faith in Him is won
Heaven's treasures which are forever new.

Those who heed Satan's tempting voice,
Who serve Him and follow his way,
Will too late know their wrong choice
And their doom in Judgment Day.

This statement is true I hasten to say
Concerning the future of man;
The wise will rejoice, the foolish pay,
For their actions concerning God's Plan.

Sometimes

Sometimes I wonder why Jesus loves me,
Why He was willing to die on that tree;
How terrible God's wrath He bids us flee
As man's years Time continually steals.

Sometimes I wonder about God's infinite grace
About His ethereal kingdom somewhere in space;
Why He would allow Jesus to die in man's place,
Which the Bible so vividly reveals.

Sometimes I wonder about God's love shown,
About future events which the Bible makes known,
Warning man to repent ere Time has flown,
For Judgment Day is near at hand.

Sometimes I wonder about a coming event
About God's actions after His patience is spent
When He will reveal again the Saviour He sent
Coming to redeem His blessed band.

Sometimes I wonder what the future will bring
To those whom to myths and fables cling,
Who deny Christ as Saviour and King,
Rejecting the only hope for man.

Sometimes I pray God to speed the day
That Christ's coming He will no longer delay
And await the promised heavenly display
When our Saviour completes God's Plan.

What More Can Our Saviour Do?

Christ Jesus made this beautiful world
The Sun is His creation too;
The azure sky our Lord unfurled,
What more can our Saviour do?

The distant stars, fashioned with grace
Christ made shining and new;
By Divine Plan each was hung in space,
What more can our Saviour do?

By omnipotent power this revolving Earth
Perfectly held in an orbit true
Has circled the brilliant Sun since birth,
What more can our Saviour do?

By Almighty God mortal man was made
And placed in a garden new;
By choice man tried God's law to evade,
What more can our Saviour do?

Mortal man lives on an island in space,
His disposition to sin God knew;
Who sent Jesus to die in man's place?
What more can our Saviour do?

Each soul on Earth must someday face
A Judgment impartial and true
To determine his eternal abiding place,
What more can our Saviour do?

The soul that on Jesus doth wholly rely
For redemption from sins old and new
Will receive from God this joyous reply:
The "Saviour" made a place for you!

Away, Soon Away

Upon this troubled island in space
Men live from day to day,
Ignorant of the redemptive grace
That's just a prayer away.

The goals for which many men seek,
The recompense they receive as pay
Are not entities which they can keep,
For Death is just a heartbeat away.

The power God allows men to hold
And the years their role holds sway
Have limits set that Time will unfold,
Which will seem just a moment away.

The peace that men should desire
Is a gift from a God of love;
The wise of this earth will aspire
To inherit God's treasures above.

Earthly wealth one day will seem
Like the shadow of a drifting cloud
And it will vanish like a dream
To the regret of the vain and proud.

The thoughts and convictions of man
His conduct and actions will sway;
Faith in Christ Jesus is God's Plan,
For redemption there's no other way.

The glory for which man does strive
Shall fade as the Sun's rays each day
And those who would be forever alive
Should trust Christ as Saviour today.

What Will Man Gain?

What will man gain if he does reach
A remote planet in outer space?
Would he then be able to teach
More about God and His grace?

What if man should reside on the Moon
And make it a stepping stone?
Would that result in a spiritual boon
Or make God's Will better known?

What if man with the speed of light
Travels the endless reaches of space?
Will that reduce his spiritual plight
And help him to seek God's face?

If man, with help from on high
Could traverse the heavens at will,
Would he tell others Salvation is nigh
Or would vanity his voice still?

I am persuaded that man will not find
God in the outer regions of space
If on Earth to God's will he is blind
And rejects God's offer of grace.

I do not know what men now seek
Beyond the bounds of this planet Earth,
But, I do know that God will not keep
Any in Heaven without their Second birth.

Let men of this planet Earth look within
Their minds, their heart and soul
And show faith in Christ Who died for sin
Whom God raised to make men whole.

The Creator's Scenes of Beauty

My eyes have seen sunsets of gold,
Rare scenes of grandeur and grace;
They have viewed mountains so old
That Time has eroded their face.

I have seen green forests tall
Whose stalwart giants seem asleep
And stood in awe as a waterfall
Spilled over a rugged precipice deep.

I've beheld the beauty of mountain lakes
Whose peace and serenity none can deny
And have been entranced by snowflakes
As they gently float through the sky.

I've seen myriad flowers growing wild
In great profusion on ridges steep;
Gently cradled by their fragrance mild,
This cherished vision I fain would keep.

I've seen the spray of the ocean tide
And rolling hills of desert sand;
I know not how long these will abide
Nor how long this Earth will stand.

I believe these creations are gifts of love
To bring Earth's mortals delight
And Christ is preparing a home above
Where He is the Source of light.

I know greater scenes are still concealed,
Which Christ will show to His Bride
When our heavenly home is revealed
And with our Lord we eternally abide.

Free

The heaven blessed mortals of Earth are free,
Free to choose a path of life to tread;
In the Holy Bible they're admonished to flee
From Satan's host of the spiritual dead.

Free to seek future rewards sublime,
Free to choose whom to serve or love,
Enjoying God's grace as He extends Time
Who offers to Believers a home above.

Free from conditions of peril in the past
Yet, facing a future uncertain and sure,
Wise mortals will seek a future that will last
Whom our loving Saviour will make secure.

Freedom of spirit and freedom of voice
Are freedoms that Earth's mortals desire;
True freedom will be gained by their right choice
Of Christ Jesus, Whom Christians love and admire.

All freedom for mortals is God's gift of love,
For His Son died in agony on the cross,
Providing for true Believers a dwelling above
Where none shall know suffering or loss.

Freedom is in Christ, Who conquered Death and Sin
And it is offered to Earth's every nation;
Repentance of sin and trusting Christ can win
Salvation for mortals whatever their station.

Free now are Earth's mortals to lose or win
Eternal Salvation, a gift beyond measure;
Those trusting Christ to save them from their sin
Will certainly have this gift to treasure.

How, What, and Who

How weak the errant pen of man,
How ineffectually does it write
When confronted by a celestial plan
That does all mortal senses delight.

What words can describe the glory
Of the golden rising Sun?
Or what pen can write the story
Of the day that Time begun?

What mind can absorb the beauty
That Nature is glad to reveal?
What conscience can escape the duty
To preserve creations with appeal?

What ear can hear the glad song
of myriad clouds in their flight?
To Whom does planet Earth belong?
Who made it a glorious sight?

What eye can pierce Night's darkness
With the clarity of Morning's light?
Who with mercy abates Winter's harshness
Expending grace with evident delight?

Who knew the corrupt tendency of mortals?
Who made The Plan to redeem the "lost"?
Who rules the Universe from heaven's portals?
Who loved enough to pay sin's dread cost?

Who knows when Christ Jesus will return
To redeem each soul trusting in Him?
The Bible reveals the fate of all who spurn
The Salvation that Christ's sacrifice did win.

Wasted Years

Aimlessly I wandered the path of life
Satisfied Satan's spoils to win;
Dissolution and discontent were rife,
The results of indulgence of sin.

I sought not God's Way or Will
As I lived from day to day,
With vanities my life I'd fill
While Satan's rule held sway.

Spirit-led one day the Saviour I sought
With my soul burdened down with sin;
And eternal change in my life was wrought
By Christ, as I professed faith in Him.

Now, today I have peace that will last
And seek not for goals that are vain;
My desire for earthly treasures is past
Since I trusted in the Lamb Who was slain.

From the narrow path may I not stray
And my love for our Saviour grow strong;
His death alone for my sin could pay
And I rejoice that to Him I belong.

It is my hope that you also shall know
The peace and security found in our Lord;
Repentant Believers faith in Christ must show
To be eternally held by Love's strong cord.

Praise be to our God in heaven above
For the eternal salvation found in His Son
Who endured Calvary's cross because of His Love
So that by faith in His Name salvation is won.

There's No One as Tolerant as God

There's nothing as permeating as God's love,
There's nothing as beautiful as a heavenly abode;
There's no one as merciful as God above
Who sent Jesus to bear mankind's sin load.

There's nothing as eternal as Heaven above,
There's nothing as wonderful as God's grace
There's nothing as sufficient as Christ's love
Who willingly died in each mortal's place.

There's nothing as powerful as God's Word
By which Salvation is brought to Earth's mortals;
The most welcome words ever to be heard
Will be the Father's greeting at Heaven's portals.

There's no one as tolerant as God
In His dealings with the inhabitants of Earth;
He remembers they were created from sod
And each needs the cherished "Second Birth."

There's no one as long-suffering toward man
As our God Who is gentle and kind,
The One Who conceived the Salvation Plan
Whom those trusting His Son can find.

There's nothing more exciting than Salvation
Which the Holy Spirit prompts mortals to receive;
Christ's sacrifice deserves a loving ovation
From those whom He has given a needed reprieve.

There will be nothing as thrilling as the sight
Of our Saviour's return from on high;
Earth's redeemed will inherit abodes of delight,
Which inheritance we hope is drawing nigh.

Our Father in Heaven

Our Father in Heaven is never asleep,
He constantly watches this planet Earth;
A continuing vigil His angels do keep
Over those of the Second Birth.

God knows mankind's wants and needs
And for their sustenance He does provide;
Even birds of the air our Father feeds
And in Nature their actions guide.

While God is thoughtful, considerate, and kind,
He desires all mortals His laws to keep;
To mankind's sinful actions He is not blind
And their cost could be unbearably steep.

This beautiful planet Earth Christ Jesus built,
It was to be mankind's heaven on earth,
Yet, sin entered Earth's mortals and their guilt
Made necessary their Second Birth.

Each soul whom his sin does truly repent
And trusts Christ Jesus as Saviour and King
Will to his peace and joy give vent
Joining other Believers Christ's praises to sing.

Life for the saved on this planet in space
May or may not be free from strife,
Yet, Christ is ever willing to dispense His grace
To those whom He has given eternal life.

Thoughts now turn to our Father above
Who has the Universe in His hand;
Believers should show Him their faith and love
And by His laws faithfully stand.

God Knows

God knows each need of mortal man;
His Son completed God's Salvation Plan;
During their lifetime each person must face
The fateful choice of a final dwelling place.

Now, God knows what the future holds;
He warns sinful man before it unfolds
That heaven is a place they must win
By faith in Christ Who forgives their sin.

God knows that there is only one Way
That mankind may share heaven's eternal day;
For opening heaven's door Christ is the Key,
To His waiting arms all Believers should flee.

God knows that men still seek another way
To inherit heaven's bright and eternal day,
Yet, God in His Holy Bible has decreed
That Christ alone can meet man's need.

God knows that man has a limited time
In which to win that prize divine;
Mortals should try to avoid Satan's evil spell
That leads the "lost" to the doom of hell.

God knows mankind's time for salvation is now
Before Time's ravages they inevitably bow;
Those seeking a future that forever will endure
Should trust in Christ Jesus to make it secure.

God knows many mortals will choose to be lost
And through Eternity will pay sin's high cost,
Yet, others will show faith in the Saviour's Name
And in heaven's glories will praise God Christ came.

The Preeminence of God

There are no words that mortals can say
To describe the preeminence of God;
Each person should follow the Saviour's Way
While on this earth he does trod.

The mortal eye has not been made
That can penetrate the reaches of space
Nor is there a soul that can evade
The penalty for refusing God's grace.

The heaven's ethereal bodies seen by man
Are awesome examples of God's powers,
Yet, the Hands that completed Creation's Plan
Are available for life's trying hours.

Yes, Christ has created celestial bodies untold,
Each hung in order in the abyss of space
And God's Holy Word does His Plan unfold,
The only plan to redeem the human race.

The mortals of Earth are not blind;
Space's countless creations they are able to see,
Yet, the Gift that each one needs to find
Is the Gift that from sin sets one free.

The only sacrifice that would suffice for man
Was Christ Jesus' death on Calvary's cross;
Our Saviour willingly died to complete God's Plan
So each Believer would escape his soul's loss.

Heaven's records will reveal each mortal's stand,
Listing those whose faith in Christ was shown;
Eternally blessed will be those in heaven's band
Whose joy will be the greatest ever known.

A Faithful Friend

As mortals tread the path of life
In the time that God is pleased to lend,
Many are beset by trouble and strife
And need the help of a faithful friend.

The only friend who can meet each need
Of the troubled mortals on this earth
Is Christ Jesus, whose open wounds did bleed
As he paid for mankind's Second Birth.

Now, Christ Jesus has for humanity paid
The price for their rescue from sin;
By trusting in His Name one can evade
His soul's loss and Salvation can win.

Christ Jesus has promised He would return
For those who have made Him their choice;
Those who reject Him and His sacrifice spurn
Are willing dupes of Satan's beguiling voice.

God's Holy Word the Bible reveals
That each mortal a choice must make;
Each should choose Jesus before Time steals
Their last opportunity Salvation to take.

Some will be wise and trust Christ as King;
They will rely on His saving power;
Through Eternity's aeons they will joyously sing,
His help was sufficient in life's trying hour.

Many others will not this decision make
To their eternal sorrow and dismay
When Hell's darkness they would forsake,
Secure in its torments they must stay.

114

God, Our Father

God, our Father, in heaven's realm above
Observes Earth's mortals with care and concern;
He makes us the object of mercy and love
Hopeful mankind His grace will discern.

God through His Son this planet has made,
Providing for mankind's legitimate needs
Although some mortals try His laws to evade,
His Spirit with sinful mankind still pleads.

God is being neglected by mortals of this Earth;
Many of whom fail to acknowledge His powers,
Few there are who seek their Second birth
Being content to waste life's precious hours.

Our God Who conceived the "Salvation Plan"
Completed by our Saviour because of His love
Offers His grace to each fallen man,
Wanting them to share heaven's mansions above.

God, our Sustainer, has a right to know
Whether Earth's mortals now accept Him as God;
Daily His blessings on man continue to flow
Although few mortals His righteous path have trod.

God whose patience mortals severely abuse
Has standards on how mankind should live;
He will dispense justice on those who refuse
The eternal salvation Christ Jesus can give.

Time, God's gift to mankind, will soon end
Bringing to the "lost" doom and dismay,
For they in hell's torments eternity will spend
While Believers will inherit heaven's eternal day.

Sometimes

Sometimes I think of God's love for me
And wonder how great His love can be,
Love that permitted His Son to die on a tree
For the sinful mortals of Earth.

Sometimes I think of Gods infinite grace,
Which was shown as Christ Jesus hung in space,
Dying on that cross in each mortal's place
Making available to Believers their Second Birth.

Sometimes I think of God's mercy shown
By making His Plan for mankind known
Ere time for their redemption had flown
And Earth's multitudes were eternally lost.

Sometimes I think of how clear the Way
Is to heaven's realm of eternal day,
Thankful under the Holy Spirit's sway
That our Saviour paid sin's dread cost.

Sometimes I wonder about the human race
Whose conduct toward God is a disgrace;
They obey not His laws nor acknowledge His grace,
Their desires are earthy at best.

Sometimes I wonder when God will give vent
To His anger when His mercy is finally spent;
Blessed will be Believers whom their sin repent
And pass this life's greatest test.

Sometimes I wonder why Salvation is free
How long God will extend His gracious plea
How many "lost" to our saviour will flee
Ere the promised Judgment Day appears.

Sometimes I wonder if maybe today
Christ's coming He will no longer delay,
Pity the "lost" under Satan's evil sway
Eternity will witness their bitter tears.

The Choice

As each new day silently slips away
Into the bottomless abyss of Eternity,
I thank god for His mercy display
And for His gifts of peace and serenity.

While sinful mankind continues to seek
Temporal blessings on this planet Earth,
I thank God that He forever will keep
Each soul that has had the Second Birth.

I ponder why God's love was shown
In His Son's death on Calvary's Cross;
By Christ's sacrifice God's grace is known
And a mortal can prevent his soul's loss.

By repentance of sin and faith in God's Son,
Life's richest blessing is available to man;
Those completing these acts salvation have won,
For this is the fruition of God's Plan.

Those foolish mortals who fail to believe
That Christ Jesus bore their sin's bitter cost,
Have no hope or chance salvation to receive
And they are among those eternally lost.

Many wise mortals to their feelings give vent,
Voicing their hope in Christ Jesus' Name,
Declaring their faith in the Saviour God sent
Trusting Jesus paid for their sin and shame.

The die has been cast and the future is sure;
Earth's mortals are still given a choice;
Believers will win a home eternal and secure
The "lost" will have no cause to rejoice.

The Return

When Christ Jesus comes in all His celestial glory
And hovers above this trembling planet Earth,
It will be the fruition of the Gospel Story
Bringing joy to those of the Second Birth.

Every mortal eye shall see Him there
As Christ His promised return shall keep;
Then the Redeemed shall rise in the air
Preceded by those who've been asleep.

This rejoicing host shall soon vanish away
To the consternation of mortals on Earth,
Whose minds cannot comprehend this display
Since they have not had their Second Birth.

Christ Jesus and His adoring host
Shall enter heaven's realm on high,
To enjoy the prize desired the most
Whose beauty all description does defy.

On planet Earth consternation holds sway
Amid speculation about what the future holds;
Lives are upset and in utter disarray
As fear and dismay of future events unfolds.

Although peace on planet Earth now reigns,
The future for its residents remains in doubt.
For each is covered with sin's dark stains
Since their chances for salvation they did flout.

Yet, hopes for their salvation still remain
While trials, troubles, and adversity pend;
Those trusting Christ as Saviour Salvation gain
And a home in Heaven where blessings never end.

Paradise Offered

Paradise is offered to mortals each day,
The Holy Bible this truth reveals;
Sadly Earth's multitudes go their own way,
Ignoring God's patient appeals.

God's message and warnings to mortals are sent
Through evangelists, preachers, and witnesses bold;
The message to the "lost" is their sin to repent
Ere speeding Time the future does unfold.

The Holy Bible God's laws for mankind reveal;
It shows why our Saviour came to this Earth;
Its message to the "lost" is they must appeal
To Christ Jesus, God's Son, for the Second Birth.

God's Holy Book tells how the saved should live,
Showing faith in Christ Jesus as Saviour and King;
Eternal blessings only our gracious God does give
Bestowed on Believers whom to His promises cling.

Today is the day God wants mortals to choose
The abode in Eternity that they really seek;
Salvation is the gift that unbelievers will lose;
Heaven's glory will be enjoyed by Believers meek.

God's grace to mankind is shown by the years
That Earth's mortals are allowed to live;
Heaven is true Paradise in the absence of tears
Containing treasures only God can give.

Where will you be when Time has expired
And God's promised Judgment takes place?
Without Salvation the lost in hell are mired
Forever to remember God's offered grace.